I0770150

GRAHAM
&
MADDIE

W. WINTERS &
AMELIA WILDE

Sealed with a Kiss

By Amelia Wilde & Willow Winters

We made a deal … one I thought I'd never make.

I'm trying not to judge myself but it's a bit shameful.
Rent was due and I simply didn't have it. I love the big city
and I've done everything I could to make it. But after a
rough few years, a breakup that nearly destroyed me, and a
personal issue that I just can't talk about…I'm broke and hit
rock bottom.
Then there's Graham.
Richer than most could ever imagine, devilishly handsome
with a charming smile, and a sparkle in his eyes that I swear
is just for me.
He owns the building, and now once a month when the rent
is due, he gets a piece of me I can't believe I agreed to give.
His lips on mine are addictive, and the way he groans my
name in pleasure is scorched into my memory.
We sealed it with a kiss, and I'm all too aware that the next
rock bottom for me will lead to nothing but despair and a
broken heart.

Sealed With A Kiss

PROLOGUE

MADDIE

Some nights are meant to be perfect, and this is one of them.

My fingers are thread through my fiancé's, Kevin's, hand as we step into the elevator in our building, my shiny new engagement ring glinting on my left hand. After a year together getting engaged is the natural—perfect—progression. We met on a blind date, moved in together three months later, and tonight he popped the question on our one-year anniversary at one of New York's most exclusive, expensive restaurants.

It could have been a scene out of a movie. Our table, with its pristine tablecloth, candles, and fine china, was completely surrounded by people who *beamed* at us, like our romance is one for the ages.

Because it *is* one for the ages. Even the waiters and

waitresses clapped for us, looking genuinely happy, and I felt a little buzzed on the complimentary champagne and cake and the *happiness.*

This is bliss. I've always been called a hopeless romantic and a decade in this city has put me through the ringer. It was all worth it though. I always knew I'd find my happily ever after.

Kevin pushes the button for our floor, his bicep flexing under my hand. A simper slips into place, and I feel the hint of a blush in my chest. I love the way he feels. The way he smells, the way he does everything.

Tonight makes the last few years feel like they've come to a close. Like I'm ready for my new chapter. I hesitate to call them bad, because that's a negative way to spin things when everything in my life has brought me to this moment.

No, they weren't bad years, but they were...challenging.

Yes. That's the right word. They were *challenging.* I went through a nasty breakup and needed a lot of late-night texting with Suzette, who's like a big sister to me. The whole situation made me feel young and naive, which in a way, I was.

Maybe I still am.

But I don't feel young and naive. I feel like a woman who's finally got her life figured out. I rose from the ashes of that boyfriend and found a man who loves me enough to marry me. I've upgraded my apartment from a teeny, tiny one-bedroom with secondhand furniture to a luxury apartment where everything's brand new and as perfect as my recent engagement. The only sign of my former life is the crocheted blanket from my grandmother, which the cleaning staff takes special care to smooth over the back of the couch every week.

The elevator lifts off with smooth acceleration.

That's probably why my stomach drops a little. It's just the elevator, not my nerves or any subconscious feeling that life can't be this good.

The future is going to be as perfect as the present. Our reflection stares back at us from the silver elevator doors. Kevin bought my wine-red dress and paid for the hair appointment that turned my dark brunette hair into gorgeous, shining waves. It feels too good to be true.

As we wait for the ding of our level, I go over my to-do list in my head, rubbing my thumb in soothing circles on his forearm. Next week, I'll refocus on my charity work. None of the positions Kevin's gotten me are paid, but they don't have to be. He told me he makes enough money that I don't have to work.

It's perfect, I remind myself again, leaning against his arm just slightly.

He doesn't lean closer to me. He's watching our reflection with a frown, like his mind is miles away. That nervous feeling comes over me again and I peer up at him, waiting for him to look back down. He doesn't.

The elevator slows, and Kevin lets out a harsh sigh. We live on the eighth floor and this is only the fourth.

"You okay?" I squeeze his arm, feeling the brand-new weight of the engagement ring on my finger.

"I just want to get home."

It takes effort for my expression to stay even and not show my shock and slight disappointment. Kevin's tone doesn't reflect a newly engaged man. I'd expected...passion, maybe. That he'd want to push me up against the wall of the elevator and kiss me until we got upstairs. I feel all these bundles of desire and want, but it's obvious he doesn't feel the same.

Kevin just sounds tired.

He seemed happy enough at the restaurant, though, so...

Maybe he *is* tired. Maybe he's desperate to get to our bedroom so he can get out of his suit and spread me out on the covers. Maybe he's as excited to continue the next phase of our perfect life as I am, he just needs a minute to collect himself.

It's good. This is good. My life is just the way I wanted it when I was living in that one-bedroom apartment, my heart aching from the breakup and my head spinning from how confused and angry I felt at my ex.

This is supposed to be the reward for coming this far. For healing my heart finding a new man and accepting everything life had to offer. This is the prize at the end of the race. I love New York City, and I love my life in it, and I've loved it hard enough to convince it to love me back.

The elevator comes to a stop on the fourth floor, and the

doors slide open to reveal a man in a suit that looks more expensive than Kevin's. It's crisp and tailored perfectly. He moves into the elevator with confident strides and takes his place next to me, then leans forward to press the button for the sixth floor. The air fills with the masculine scent of his cologne and all it takes is one inhale.

One single breath and I'm drawn to him. I can't help stealing a glance in the reflection. He's tall, with dark hair and carved features. As he straightens from pushing the button, his eyes catch mine. They're so blue—*so* blue that my breath catches.

I look away, my pulse racing. This isn't how a woman is supposed to feel about a man who isn't her fiancé. I'm not falling in love with him. It's not one of those fairy-tale scenarios. I'm past believing in those.

But I can't bring myself to look away. My eyes keep finding him in the reflection.

The elevator glides upward again. My heart races and I chide myself for feeling anything in the slightest.

We only have a few moments together. The elevators in this building are fast, and he's only going up two floors. I try to make it seem like I'm not staring, but I am, and that's how I notice when he looks at me.

His eyes linger on my body in the reflection, trailing down the dress Kevin bought for me.

Any thoughts of him are a mistake. I shut them down

quickly, holding onto Kevin's arm with both hands.

Because the moment I tear my eyes off the stranger, I become aware of Kevin watching both of us with a clenched jaw. Kevin dislodges my hold on his arm and puts his hand on the small of my back.

His possessiveness takes me by surprise but I lean into it. Staring straight ahead as if the man isn't even here.

I do not want any part of being kissed or touched by a stranger in a nice suit who happens to have one of the most gorgeous faces I've ever seen.

My face gets hot at my imagined fantasy of this stranger kissing me in the way I wish Kevin would. That's all it is—a fantasy. A short, unasked-for fantasy that's only happening because of the champagne and the excitement of the evening.

That's all. I clear my throat and shake the odd thoughts off, ignoring the prying eyes I swear I can still feel on me.

The elevator stops, and the man next to me shifts his weight to leave.

His elbow brushes against mine.

The fabric of his suit brushes against my bare elbow and it feels as sensual as a kiss, almost as intimate as one. He didn't have to touch me—there's room in the elevator for him to get in and out with zero contact—but he did, and it's electric.

What's going on with me? Electricity over a man's suit?

He turns his head as he reaches the doors. "Good night."

His voice matches his impeccable suit and his gorgeous

face. It's low and rich and somehow, deep in my bones, sounds familiar.

"Good night," Kevin snaps.

The other man doesn't seem to notice the bite in Kevin's tone. As the doors begin to close, he turns to go down the hall and looks back in at me. His eyes are still locked on mine when the doors shut completely, cutting me off from him.

He was an attractive man, and I couldn't help but notice. He doesn't have anything to do with me and Kevin.

He doesn't.

"What a prick," Kevin mumbles under his breath.

I actually don't think we can fault the man for using the same elevator, but I don't say that. I slip my hand into Kevin's instead.

"Don't worry about him." I smile up at my new fiancé. "Think about us. This is our big night."

"You're right about that." He turns my hand in his and runs the pad of his thumb over my ring. "You're mine now."

"Now?" I joke. "Wasn't I yours before? Or does it only count once we've made vows?"

Kevin frowns, not even giving me a courtesy laugh.

The elevator takes us up the remaining floors, and I step close to him and try to communicate that everything is normal. Better than normal. It's the start of our forever.

There's always a comedown when you do something special, right? The adrenaline fades. Soon we'll be in bed together, and the guy in the elevator won't matter at all.

I'm not going to think about him again.

I don't think about him when the elevator doors open, or when Kevin takes us inside the apartment. I don't think about him while I slip into the lingerie I put on Kevin's card earlier this morning. I don't think about him when Kevin takes me to bed and we have fast, perfunctory sex that unfortunately doesn't do the trick.

I don't think about him when I'm lying on the pillows afterward, Kevin already breathing deeply beside me.

I really don't think about him. Not his blue eyes, not the way his suit fit on his body, and not the way he brushed his arm against my elbow like he just had to touch me, even if it was through his clothes.

I don't think about him at all when I lift up my hand in the dark and watch the diamond catch the tiniest glimmers of light.

I don't think about him when I find the texts on Kevin's phone a week later.

I don't think about him when the woman comes to confront me a few days after that.

I don't think about him when my world falls apart and I'm left feeling foolish and naive and alone again.

All I think about is how well and truly fucked I am and how my happily ever after turned into a nightmare.

CHAPTER 1

GRAHAM

Sometimes, when I'm on my way back from a business meeting, I stop across the street from the luxury apartments I own and take it all in.

It's a modern building. Clean. A wrought-iron fence surrounds a narrow lawn out front with a bricked-in path leading to the doors adding old city charm. All of it is tended by a team of landscapers who maintain the property daily. I'm not the person who built it from the ground up, but I bought it and made it mine.

On afternoons like this one, the building represents the epitome of my success. It would have been a dream come true for my parents to see how far I've come. They didn't grow up with money and when I first saw this place it reminded me of a make-believe house my mother used to say we would have one day. My father worked too hard for too little and died too young to enjoy it. My mom couldn't bear to live without him. Once I was alone in the world, I swore I wouldn't have that kind of life.

I wouldn't settle for just getting by.

The apartments should be proof that I've more than reached those goals. Everything about them is meant to remind people that they're home, and that home is somewhere important. That's why the front facade is pristine and white. That's why the windows shine in the sun. That's why plants rise above the rooftop.

It means everything to me.

Or at least it should.

But sometimes, when I'm coming back from a business meeting, I look at the building and think I have a hell of a long way to go before I'll feel like I've made it.

Today's one of those days.

A lunch meeting about a property I'm hoping to acquire ran long. I don't have a good feeling about how things are going, which only makes me more determined to see it through. It's twice as large as the luxury apartment building that's been my personal pet project for the last five years, and it will mean leveling up.

Though some part of me wonders what's next *after* that. Some part of me is already looking ahead to even bigger things. There's never enough. There's never a stopping point.

Right now, I'm separated from the building—technically, my home—by two lanes of traffic. The cars move past in a steady stream. For a moment, I could be anyone at all. A stranger in New York City. I could be the man I was ten years ago, staring at buildings like this and swearing I'd get there someday. I'd own a penthouse here.

Now I own more than one building, but something's still missing.

There's an emptiness no amount of money can fill, and it's more and more apparent every passing day.

With my gaze moving to the yellow light, I wait for the traffic to stop before I cross. The sidewalk in front of my building is busy. A couple passes by me, focused on each other, and I look away.

My mind wanders back to the woman in the elevator.

I haven't stepped into an elevator in six months without thinking of her.

The woman. Dark hair. Dark eyes. A look in her eyes that I haven't forgotten. A red dress that clung to every curve on her body like it was made just for her. For all I know, it was.

She was standing in the elevator with another man, which should have been enough to make me forget her instantly. Immediately. I don't fuck with women who are already involved with someone else, certainly none who have a ring on their finger.

Lucky for me, remembering a person isn't the same as getting involved with them.

It would be convenient if I could stop thinking about her, though. If I could stop thinking of the way her eyes met mine in the reflection of the gleaming door. I felt something just from her dark eyes on mine. Sensed something in the air. Her perfume had been all around her, and it made me want to do something crazy. Something like…lean in and kiss the side of her neck even while she had her hand on another man's arm.

He was nothing compared to her. Even the way her breath hitched was fascinating.

I've thought about the way her breasts rose and fell underneath her dress every damn day for six months. Like whatever had come over me was felt by her as well.

Attempting to rid her of my mind and ignoring the fact that I have to ride that damn elevator again, that it may have hints of her perfume if she's ridden it today, I stride into my building.

I head into the lobby, scanning to make sure everything's as it should be. Custom tiled flooring is polished and shining. Custom sconces on the walls have every bulb burning. The doormen behind the desk are properly uniformed and both of them nod to me as I go by.

It's the weekend, but I'm headed back to my office, not to the penthouse. I don't want to stand in the elevator and think about her. Beyond that, my personal space is as luxurious as the rest of the building. Obviously—I wouldn't settle when it came to that, either.

Sometimes, despite all the high-end furnishings and the professional kitchen and the miles of extra space, it still feels empty.

I could have my pick of dates and outings, but after a meeting like that one, I'm not in the mood.

My office space on the fifth floor is lit from the outside. I'm not planning to turn on any lights. I'm barely past my secretary's desk when my phone buzzes in my pocket.

The number on the screen is an unfamiliar one. It could be one of the people from the meeting, wanting to continue the conversation, and my pulse pumps harder at the thought. I could tackle some of this bullshit today. Find my footing as far as the deal goes.

I accept the call. "Graham Maxwell."

"Hi," a woman says. She wasn't at the meeting. Her voice heats something low in my torso. "I mean—hello, Mr. Maxwell. My name is Madelyn Cunnigham. I live on the eighth floor of your West Grove apartments."

I stare out my office windows, hardly seeing the cityscape outside. "I think you're looking for the building manager, Ms. Cunnigham."

"No. No. I was looking for you."

"Were you?" I entertain the conversation for no other reason than because *that* woman lived on the eighth floor. I allow myself to imagine it's her, although I'm careful with my thoughts. I'm more giving than I should be.

"Yes. I was hoping to have a conversation." My gaze drops as her tone turns with slight desperation. "The building manager sent me your way as...I'm having a difficulty I am hoping you could help me with. If you had a few minutes. I wouldn't take up much of your time, I promise."

"Something wrong with your apartment? A broken appliance? Because I can direct you to the weekend maintenance team."

"All the appliances are fine, but there's a slight emergency."

I move closer to my desk in case this woman with the beautiful voice has panicked and called *me* instead of the fire department.

"Fire? Flood?"

"Neither of those," she says quickly. "Nothing's on fire. I just wanted a conversation. I need to have a conversation with you." I like the way *need to have a conversation with you* sounds. "I could meet you in your office or...or anywhere, really. I'm right upstairs. I can be ready on a moment's notice."

"How about this? I'll come to you." I have no idea what's happening here, but I intend to find out. "Which unit are you in?"

"Unit 8A."

"All right." I pull the chair out from behind my desk. "Are you sure you don't need the fire department?" I attempt to add a touch of humor to ease her concerns.

"I'm completely sure," she promises.

"Give me five minutes."

"Okay. Thank you so…thank you. I'll be here."

The call disconnects, and I tap my password into my computer. I'm not going up to the eighth floor without some basic information in my back pocket.

I have the lease agreement in a few clicks. Not much here. There's Madelyn's name listed underneath a guy named Kevin. My stomach sinks, but I ignore that. I don't have any reason to be disappointed. I liked the sound of her voice. That's all. The odds that she's the woman in the red dress are low I tell myself. There are thirty-some apartments on that level.

Now I have no choice but to think about the woman in the elevator. She's a welcome distraction from thinking about this woman on the phone.

I go out and push the call button.

There're plenty of other things to occupy my mind. I own properties all over New York City. None compare to this building, which is my pride and joy, but they all add to the considerable balances in my bank accounts.

I'm richer by the second. Money piles up even as I step into the elevator and hit the button for the eighth floor.

The doors close and I can almost see her there in that dress, with those hooded eyes. If she stood just behind me, most of her body would be hidden by mine. If I turned around to touch her...

I'm not thinking about this. I'm not thinking about some mystery woman, who lives in this building that I own, with whoever the hell was in the elevator with her that night.

The elevator stops at the eighth floor and the doors open. One of the doormen is waiting in the hall and he steps back with a deferential nod. "Mr. Maxwell."

"Tom."

He waits for me to exit, then takes my place in the elevator.

I'm alone in the hall. Compared to how loud the city is, even a space like this—a hallway meant to take people from place to place and not much more—feels luxurious. I made sure it was that way. I insisted on plush carpeting, crown molding, and neutral paint colors with a hint of warmth. This place isn't institutional. This is a home for people who need an escape. An oasis.

The only person it's not an escape for is me.

I own the building. I headquarter my business here. I live in the penthouse. There's not a square inch of this building that's meant for anything but making money, and that's what I intend to do. Double it. Triple it. Become so unfathomably rich that I can forget about my past entirely and never have worries or burdens like the ones I grew up with, the ones that put my father into an early grave.

And this...this isn't an errand that will make me any money.

I don't pay house calls. I have people for that.

Today, I'm making an exception.

That's her door. 8A.

I raise my hand and knock, not expecting to see her there. Staring wide-eyed at me in a simple yet elegant red dress like we're back in that elevator.

Fuck me.

CHAPTER 2

MADDIE

This is it.

This is *it*.

I move quickly through the apartment and call out, "I'm coming," in what I hope is a calm, confident voice. I'm definitely not calm or confident. That means faking it is my only option.

I take a deep breath and open the door, not prepared for a wave of air to be pulled from my lungs.

Graham Maxwell is gorgeous. That's the first thought that comes to mind. He's tall and dark haired with the kind of face that belongs in the movies. Blue eyes that look me up and down with a kind of heated curiosity. The sight of him makes my heart race and my palms sweaty.

"Oh!" I blurt out, because...oh my God. It's him—the man from the elevator. I'm reminded of that night all over again. And then the pain that happened afterward. "We've met before. Or...I saw you in an elevator before."

He flashes me a smile that's all charm. He is a million times more confident than I am when he offers me his hand to shake. "Graham Maxwell."

I take it, immediately overwhelmed by how solid and strong it feels. His touch is hot and I have to pull my hand away sooner than I'd like. I slip my hand out of his, concentrating hard on keeping my breathing steady. "Maddie."

"Maddie," he murmurs my name, like he's testing it out. The way he says it is nearly sinful.

That buzz between us is still there. I can *feel* it, just like I felt it for those thirty seconds in the elevator six months ago.

"Please. Come in. Can I offer you anything to drink?" I swallow thickly, attempting to calm myself down. I keep telling myself it'll be okay even if this doesn't work out, but I know it's a lie. I need him to help me, or the downward spiral of my life is going to get even worse.

"I think we'd better cut to the chase." His voice makes it hard to think. "On the phone, you said you had an...urgent problem to discuss."

My face gets hot. I knew what I was asking for when I made that phone call. Actually having him in my apartment is overwhelming. "Let's sit down. Is that okay?"

He hesitates; his hands find their way into his suit pockets. I watch his Adam's apple as he swallows, and I admire the way the cords in his neck tighten. Every inch of him could be cut from marble. "Lead the way."

I take him to the living room and tuck myself into a loveseat. Mr. Maxwell takes the armchair across from me. His scent fills the room—the same hint of expensive cologne as before. I remember it.

"The emergency," he prompts.

I square my shoulders. "Right. Yes. First, I wanted to apologize for the inconvenience. I know you're very busy."

"It's nothing. Tell me what's wrong."

My face gets even hotter. "I'd like to speak to you about the rent."

"The rent for this apartment?"

"I'm sure, in a place like this…" Why didn't I plan this speech out before I called him? "I know you're probably not the one people come to about problems like this, but it's the weekend. I was up all night." Anxiousness sweeps a heat over my entire body. I can barely breathe knowing the weight of this conversation.

He studies me. "What's the problem with the rent?"

"I can't pay it." I'm quick to correct myself. "I can't pay all of it." *Deep breaths, Maddie.* "This is my home, it's the only thing I have right now, and I can't quite cover the rent for this month."

"Your husband can't cover it?" he asks, and it's like a knife to the chest.

I twist my hands together out of habit, and his eyes drop to my fingers then snap back to my face.

"He wasn't my husband, actually," I tell him. "He was my fiancé, but he's not anymore. We're over. He left."

"Without leaving enough money to cover the rent?" He lets out a disbelieving laugh. "The kind of people who live in this building have second homes in Europe."

"He was that kind of person. He was going to be, anyway, but I'm not." Okay. Here it comes. "I hope you know that this isn't a long-term problem. I have a plan to fix it, I just need more time because I wasn't prepared for this. If I go to him, I'm sure he'll simply end the lease, and there's nothing around here that I can afford and that's available. I've been off the market for a couple of years, so it's taking me longer than I thought to find a job that can pay enough. I've gone through my savings, and I've sold most everything I could."

"Off the market?"

"Out of the job market. My ex thought it would be better for his career if I focused on philanthropy instead of building my own career, so that's what I did. And I don't regret it. I helped a lot of people, but I'm at a loss at the moment. I paid everything but the five hundred and everyone said that I needed to talk to you."

His blue eyes are absolutely captivating. "What's the exact situation with the rent, Maddie? You can't afford any of it?"

"No, I can afford most of it. I'm five hundred dollars short. And I'll give you anything you want to cover it."

I'm shocked at the words that have just come out of my mouth, but I mean it. I'm solving this problem. I don't care what it takes. I've sold almost all my jewelry in the past months to make it work. I can't even afford to break this lease now. I don't know what else to do.

"*Anything*," I insist. My heart races.

Graham Maxwell looks at me across my living room, his eyes going dark. "We can come to an arrangement."

Relief hits me like a gust of fresh air. "Oh, thank you. Thank you so much. What kind of arrangement?"

"I have an idea," he says as his eyes drop to my breasts, and I have to admit, I want it. If that's what he wants, I wanted it anyway. Before I can stop myself, I agree to what he's suggesting.

"If you want me, you can have me however you'd like."

He pauses, almost as if he's stopped breathing and embarrassment lights my cheeks aflame. But that look in his eyes lights a different part of me ablaze.

"What exactly is it that you have in mind?"

"I think...I'm not sure. I haven't..."

A moment passes and then he asks, "A quick fuck then?"

I gasp in spite of myself. I've been nervous about what he might say, but I never expected him to say it like *this*.

Although, if I'm being truthful, I love the tension between

us. I love the way it felt to meet his eyes in the elevator. And if this is what it takes, if I get to experience a fantasy I had…I'm more than willing.

"You really want me?" I whisper the question and wonder if I'm merely daydreaming.

"From the moment I saw you in that elevator."

"Oh my God."

"You wanted me, too," he guesses as he spreads his legs a bit wider, and my gaze drops to the bulge in his pants. I'm instantly hot.

I bring my hands up to cover my face, then comb my fingers through my hair and look back up at him. "Yes," I admit. "I did."

"Then take your clothes off, and you can stop worrying about the rent."

My heart races. "I…" I did say *anything*.

"You don't have much time," he adds. He looks hungry now. Almost desperate. "No doubt you've spent all weekend trying to collect the money with no success. So let's do this instead." I stare wide-eyed back at him, knowing this is my only chance to back out and if I do… well I don't know what I'll do. "I've wanted you for months, Madelyn. I'll make it good for you. I'll make sure you enjoy yourself."

I close my eyes. My heart beats and beats a steady *thud*.

Then I open them and get to my feet.

My shirt is the first thing to go. Then the bodysuit I'm

wearing underneath.

"Stop," he says.

I freeze. Graham Maxwell gets up from his seat and comes around the table to me, his eyes raking over every inch of my skin covered only by my bra and panty set. His breath turns heavier as he unbuttons his shirt.

Then his hands are on my waist, gentle but firm.

"Fucking gorgeous," he murmurs.

"You're gorgeous yourself," I say, feeling drunk on how close he is with his palms on my waist. His touch is electrifying and it's in this moment I know I'm going to remember this forever.

"Birth control?" he asks, and I nod. "Have you been tested since—"

"Yes. You?" He nods. "Good."

He lets out a groan and peels off my panties and bra in quick movements. Then his mouth is on the side of my neck, and I—

I can't think about anything but how good his lips feel.

I tilt my head back to give him better access, and he takes full advantage, leaving opened mouthed kisses that force me to moan from the instant pleasure.

And then—it's like he reaches some breaking point. Mr. Maxwell maneuvers me over to the arm of the sofa, the pad of his thumb brushing over one of my nipples. I let out a soft sound. It feels so damn good to be touched. To be wanted. I wish I could live in this moment. After the hell of what I've been through, I need this.

With firm guidance, he turns me around and bends me over, forcing a gasp from me.

"Fuck. Your thighs are perfect." His voice is low and rough. He slides a hand between my legs and nudges them apart, then finds my wet slit with his fingertips. When he finds my clit, I can't help the moan that comes out of my mouth.

Graham curses again, his fingers working faster on my clit. I hear the sounds of his zipper and of fabric moving, and then he's working me harder while the tip of his cock nudges against my opening.

"Yes," I tell him. "Fuck me. Please fuck me."

It's filthy to beg a man this way, but Graham likes it. He makes another primal sound from deep in his chest and pushes himself inside me.

His cock fills me and pushes me to the brink of pain, and it forces another gasp out of me. He's so fucking big. He stops, buried inside of me, and lets me adjust. It takes a moment, while I hold my breath, for the sting of being stretched to be eased by the pleasure. I spread my thighs a little wider and rock back against him, lost in the feeling of being completely filled by a man for the first time in months.

Graham doesn't hesitate. The second I move against him, he fucks into me hard, then harder. Between his fingers and his body, I'm drowning in pleasure.

"Oh," I gasp. "Oh, oh—"

"Come on my cock," he orders in a breathy tone at the shell of my ear. "That's what I want for the rent."

That statement alone nearly makes me come undone. I think about how I'm a little whore for him. How the perverse act is a fantasy come to life.

I let out another moan and come undone. My fingernails scrape against the couch cushions as I try to brace myself.

"That's a good girl," he praises me as he rides through my orgasm.

With one broad hand on my lower back, he comes inside of me. I can feel every bit of his heat pulsing inside me. Everywhere. Holy shit. My eyes widen as I'm brought back down from the highest of highs.

His thrusts slow, but it's a long minute before he pulls out and helps me up.

As he offers me his hand when my legs take a moment to stabilize, I can hardly believe it's done. He kept his word. It was a quick fuck. A damn good quick fuck that left me wanting more.

"That was," I start to tell him and have to catch my breath as he hands me my shirt. "That was really good."

My eyes meet his and I catch his smirk. "You were incredible," he tells me, and I have to look away as I dress myself. A mix of emotions swarms over me.

"Do you need anything?" he asks, and I only shake my head.

He puts himself back together, faster than I could have imagined. His eyes burn over my body, and I wonder for an instant what he's hiding behind them. "Don't worry about the five hundred dollars. We're even."

Graham Maxwell sees himself out of my apartment but not before turning and telling me that if I need anything at all not to hesitate to ask.

Technically, it's *his* apartment. He's the man who owns this building and has the power to kick me out if I don't pay rent, and he's also the man I've just had sex with to cover the shortfall.

Oh my God. I've just had sex with the owner of the building to pay the rent.

Did I...like that?

Did I *love* it?

I still feel buzzed from the way he fucked me, his strokes deep and possessive. It's been a long time since I was with a man who took me like that. He took me like he owned me and fucked the shit out of me. That's exactly what Graham did. I don't think it *ever* happened that way with Kevin, or any of my other exes for that matter.

My heart races. Graham isn't even in the room anymore, and I'm still feeling the effects.

I sweep up the clothes from the living room floor and walk on shaky legs to the bathroom where I toss them into the hamper. I turn on the shower without thinking, wait for the water to get hot, and climb in.

"I just paid the rent with sex," I say out loud, just to test it out.

My whole body feels like it's blushing, but I don't feel ashamed.

Should I feel ashamed?

No, right? I didn't do anything wrong. Two consenting adults. A business arrangement sort of...for rent.

"Oh, God, I *loved* it," I admit to the empty shower.

They're really two separate things. I needed to come up with five hundred dollars for this month's rent, and I needed to get over Kevin. I've spent months in a panic, trying to find a job and failing, waking up all night freaking out about the future.

I wondered if I could have done something else to make us work. But it wasn't *me* in the end. It was him. He found someone else, cheated for months, and left once I found out. He wanted to have his cake and eat it too. I'm still not over the heartache entirely, mostly because it proves just how naive I am.

It's hard to feel hung up on past mistakes after the way Graham touched me though.

Mr. Maxwell?

I don't know what to call him, but that's okay. This won't happen again. I'll find a job and fix my life, and I won't have to have sex with anyone to pay the rent ever again. I was acting out a fantasy. One that paid well. But I will never do that again.

Even if I did like it.

Even if I did come *hard* while he was inside me. I came on his cock like he told me to. I've never been talked to like that. Not once. And I loved it.

That didn't happen with Kevin. I never came that hard. I'm more ashamed of the fact that I used to wait until he fell asleep and get myself off under the covers so I didn't hurt his feelings. How did I ever accept that as my normal life when something so much better was out there?

I take a deep breath of hot steam, pushing the wet hair from my face, and let it out.

He seemed stable and kind. That's why I was with Kevin. He was so nice...so nice that I didn't see through the lies and the cheating. I've been through bad breakups before, and I thought my relationship with him was the next step in my life. I thought I was leaving behind all those unpredictable men and finally growing up.

I'm not going to blame myself for that.

I'm not going to downplay the memories of Graham, either.

I shake my head under the hot water, unable to stop imagining what just happened. That felt *good*. It felt *amazing*. Maybe it shouldn't have. Maybe I should have demanded that he buy me dinner and roses before we had sex. Kevin did all those things for me. He bought bouquets of roses and took me out to dinner and asked me to marry him...and he left.

But I didn't want those things in the moment. I wanted

a quickie with the guy from the elevator with fuck-me eyes.

I'm *not* going to get hung up on either Kevin or Graham. That's not what I'm going to do.

I focus back on the shower. I'm not in any hurry to get the scent of his cologne off my skin. I mostly came here as a matter of habit, but I regret it a little as I'm soaping up my skin. I can still feel the places he touched me. He wasn't rough. He was firm, though. Like he already knew me. Like I already belonged to him.

Except this was never about belonging to anybody. It was just to pay the rent.

I keep convincing myself of that as I get out of the shower and get dressed. I feel like I've just woken up from a deep, refreshing sleep, and my mind is clear for the first time since my ex left.

Is that what happens when you're with a person who understands you? Because it felt like Graham understood me.

I might not know much about the man, but I understood what he needed from me in that moment. *Needed.* That was right there in his eyes. I pause, the towel wrapped around me, in front of the mirror that's edged with steam. Hopeless romantics get their hearts broken. Suzette told me that just last week over red wine and another hard cry.

I need to stop these thoughts. I need to focus on the task at hand.

I shut down all thoughts as I get ready and get back to

emails and resumés intent on finding a job and writing Graham off as a one-time divulgence.

That's the plan, anyway, until my phone buzzes on the kitchen counter. I hear the soft hum from my walk-in closet and dash out through the apartment in bare feet. It's too big a place for one person with two bedrooms, two bathrooms, an office, and a breakfast nook. But I've done the math on getting a new place on short notice. I was five hundred dollars short on this rent. I don't have enough to cover a deposit on another place, either, unless I have roommate.

I reach the phone and snatch it up from the countertop without looking at the screen.

"Hello?"

"Maddie, it's me."

"Kenzie! How are you?" My heart speeds up again at the sound of my cousin's voice. I love Kenzie to death, but her life is even more precarious than mine was before I met Kevin. "Everything okay?"

"Not really," she says with a sigh. "I need help."

"Oh, Kenzie," I can't hide the strain in my voice. My stomach sinks. I want to be in a position to help my cousin any time she calls, but I'm not. I used to be, and I will be again, but right now? I can't even help myself.

I'm hoping all she needs is to talk things over.

"I didn't want to have to call you," she continues. "But I don't have any other choice."

"What's due?" I ask, pacing out of the kitchen and back to the big picture windows in the living room.

"My student loans."

My cousin never made it to graduation. She had a hard time the first two years of college. It wasn't easy for her to settle on a major. She went through three student advisers, and all suggested she get a different degree. Now she's part way through two separate majors and three minors and hasn't taken classes in a year. The student loan companies won't let her off the hook. She's young and in severe debt.

"When?" I ask automatically.

"The fifteenth."

"Then you still have two weeks to work it out, right?"

"I'm not going to get there." I can hear the panic in her voice, though she tries to hide it. "I'm behind on other bills, too. Had to cover those with my savings so the electricity didn't get turned off."

I hate the sound of that. I don't want my cousin—my family—to be in a position where she can't afford basic necessities. She already works two jobs. Waitressing doesn't always make ends meet. Today is a perfect example of that.

"Kenzie." I try to sound as calm and reasonable as I can. "Are you sure you don't want to—"

"Don't say I should move in with you, Maddie. I don't have the cash for that, either. It's just too far."

This is the worst part about Kevin leaving. Looking back,

it's obvious that I wasn't happy with him. He wasn't going to be in love with me no matter how hard I tried. That's a tough lesson to keep learning from men, and I'm determined not to have to learn it again.

But at least when we were together, money was no object. I could send Kenzie what she needed to get by and hope that it would be enough to get her where she needed to go.

Ugh. I wish I'd ignored him about quitting my job. My grandmother was right when she told me to keep a separate savings account and build it up as much as I could. If I'd followed her advice, I wouldn't need help covering the rent.

Then again, Graham Maxwell never would have come to my apartment. My thighs tighten and I have to close my eyes and shut down the memory.

"Kenz, I really, really want to be the person you can count on," I begin.

She huffs a sigh, and I know it's out of disappointment and desperation. I know that *exact* feeling because that's how I felt when I woke up this morning. It's probably a pipe dream to think that I'll ever live a worry-free life.

"I just can't cover this month. I'm sorry. I barely made the rent."

"I don't get it." Traffic goes by in the background, making her voice sound even shakier than it is. My heart hurts for her. I know what it's like to be on your own with your life constantly on the brink. "What went so wrong with Kevin?"

"He cheated on me. You know that's what happened."

"Couldn't you have—"

"Couldn't I have done *what?*" This day has been a rollercoaster, and now I'm heading up another high hill, frustrated as all get out. I'm guilty of blaming myself for Kevin leaving but hearing it from another person reminds me that it's bullshit. "Convinced him not to cheat? Been better somehow? I did everything he asked me to do."

"I know, I know," she says, softening. "I'm sorry. I didn't mean to accuse you of anything, I just—"

"It's fine. It'll be okay," I tell Kenzie. "All of this will work out. We just have to—"

"Keep trying?" My cousin lets out a bitter laugh. "I knew you'd say that. I gotta go. I'm almost at work."

"Okay, but—"

She hangs up before I can finish my sentence and the guilt weighs heavy in my chest.

"I'll always be here for you," I shout at the phone. "That's what I was going to say. I'll be here for you, I just don't have the *money* you need." Tears sting the corner of my eyes and my throat goes dry.

I whirl away from the window, frustrated beyond belief, and as I do, the phone flies out of my hand.

It tumbles through the air in slow motion and hits the window much harder than I thought it would.

It hits the window so hard that it cracks. All the blood drains from my face and my hands go cold.

"No!" I shout, and rush to the window. The phone's landed on the floor with only a minor scuff on the case, but the window has a crack in it.

A crack. In the giant picture window. *Shit.*

Shit, shit, shit.

How the hell am I going to pay for this?

CHAPTER 3

GRAHAM

Another day, another meeting.

More stress.

All the while, my mind wandered.

The man I've been meeting with, Harland Porter, is throwing up roadblock after roadblock to the sale. Concern after concern. Question after question. I don't know why he put the damned property up on the market if he's so obsessed with it.

I'm not obsessed with any property like that.

Although, my mind drifting once again, I'm a bit concerned I may be becoming obsessed with Madelyn.

Obsession has no place in a deal like that.

I can't stop thinking about her. It was one fuck, so it

shouldn't mean anything. I'm the one who was in charge of the situation. I could've offered anything and I offered that deal, and she *wanted* it. I run my hand over the back of my neck as Harland drones on and my business associates answer.

It takes great effort to keep my expression stern and unmoving as my thumb runs over the tip of my pointer and I imagine her soft skin and delectable moans.

Years ago, I thought that being filthy rich would solve all my problems. It hasn't. It solved some of them, that's for sure. I won't ever have to worry about losing my house or being on the street. I won't ever be in the position of begging someone for rent money.

Those concerns are far behind me, and the ones that are ahead have much higher stakes. People work for me now. People depend on me. Which means it's not just me I have to think about when it comes to making these deals.

It might be easier if I had something to take the edge off. Something real and constant in my life other than my penthouse apartment. What my apartment has going for it is that it's predictable. It's expensive and luxurious, decorated exactly to my taste, and nobody else ever interferes. It offers me privacy and an escape. But it's hollow and far too quiet.

For the second time this week, I catch myself thinking about what it would be like to come home to *someone*, not just *some place*.

Not a wife. I can't imagine marriage. And not a girlfriend...

I'm not interested in complications and emotions.

All that is a distraction. I know what happens to men who fall too deep into finding that missing someone. Statistics on love and marriage are far too telling. The majority of people never find 'the one' and end up alone. Half of those who do take the leap into love end up unhappy and broke after divorce.

"Let's take five?" Harland questions and the associates agree. The computer screen shows them all nodding, and I agree to the short break. Once the camera is off, I rub a hand over my face and lean back in my chair. I click over the tabs to another long email chain. We've been going back and forth for an hour. Part of me wants to cut my losses and stop spending time trying to acquire a property that's not truly available.

What would it say about me if I invested all this time and walked away with nothing? It would say that I wasn't up to the challenge. It would say I could be deterred by a few annoying emails.

Nobody's ever going to be able to say that about me. If they say anything, they'll say that I was too determined. That I wouldn't stop at anything to get what I wanted. If this business has taught me one thing it's that patience is immeasurable.

I respond to Porter's latest email and click over to the app for the building's security system. A window showing twelve small rectangles, each with the view from a separate camera, pops up on the screen. This, unlike working on the acquisition, gives me a sense of peace. I can see that everything is how it should be in the parking area. A delivery man taps away at his tablet at the back entrance, then jogs back to his truck, climbs in, and drives away. In the lobby, an older tenant chats with the doorman, who looks like he's explaining something to her, his hands flying.

This is the place I've made through my money and my effort and my force of will.

I've built something to be proud of, something that runs smoothly and provides for others, but that doesn't mean there's nothing else I want in my life. It doesn't mean I don't have other goals. My heart speeds up, stress spreading across my shoulders and back. What I want is something physical—a trip to the gym or a run, something to let my muscles work.

What I want is Maddie.

How does she fit in to a life like mine? I can't be the man who never gives up on anything if I want her and don't go after her. I can't be the man who goes after her and keeps his eyes on the prize at the same time.

It's like she hears my thoughts, or the universe does, because the instant her name enters my mind, a woman walks into view of one of the security cameras.

It's her, crossing the street to the building. She tucks a lock of dark hair behind her ear and waits for traffic to stop. Then she strolls into the sidewalk, looking gorgeous and elegant in heels and a dress that hugs her hips and shows off her collarbone with a square neckline that makes me want to stick my hand underneath it just to feel the softness of her skin.

Maddie is completely put together as she moves across the white painted lines on the road. She flashes the drivers in the cars a perfect smile and gives them a little wave to thank them for stopping.

I'm hard just looking at her. Out there, in public, she looks lovely and demure. She *is* lovely and demure. But I know how she sounds when she's bent over a piece of furniture and moaning for my cock. I know how wet it makes her to come to filthy secret agreements with a man with money—very, very wet. And *fuck*, it's hot. That damned voice in my mind tries to remind me that there's so much more than raw sexual desire. There's so much more I could give her beyond a few hundred dollars and a quickie.

I'm not going to go there right now. I take a deep breath and adjust myself in my pants. A more decent guy would turn off the security app, but I'm not exactly interested in being a decent man when it comes to this situation.

Maddie strides into the building, smiles at the doorman, and says something to him. My brow creases as a touch of possessiveness overwhelms me. It's unexpected and my finger hovers on the key to turn the camera off. Tom is a trustworthy man, otherwise I wouldn't have hired him, but another man's eyes on her makes my stomach knot with jealousy.

I can't even *be* jealous. She's not mine.

She's just beautiful and holds a spark I haven't felt from anyone else.

If there was a woman waiting for me in my apartment at the end of every day, I'd want her to be Maddie.

Fuck. I can't think like that. What we have isn't anything long-term or deep, no matter how much I think I want that.

I dig my fingernails into the arm of my office chair to keep myself in the damn seat. Maddie has every right to walk into the lobby of my building, where *she* lives, and talk to the doorman. She has every right to talk to whoever she wants. She doesn't belong to me.

Just when I've finally fucking lost it and started to get up from the chair, Maddie turns away from the reception desk. For a split second, I can see her face before she heads for the elevators. The kind smile that she wore into the lobby drops away into a worried frown.

I pause. Concern spreading through my veins.

What's that about?

My computer pings with a message that the meeting has ended. I click over to the meeting tab. Harland apologizes but something has come up and he'll email once he's available again. Irritation spreads through me but I remind myself: patience.

I click both windows closed, get up from my seat, and go to the floor-to-ceiling window. My only thoughts are of

Madelyn and how to approach her again. It was expression on her face. There's no way I can tell her I was watching her on the cameras—that would be an invasion of privacy, and she'd never want to fuck me again.

Which isn't the only thing I'm worried about.

I'm worried about *her*. I'm worried that some serious problem worries her. I don't care for it.

As I stare down at the bustling streets, I debate on how to handle her. I can go knock on her door and make sure everything's fine. Maddie came to me with a problem. It would be a gentlemanly thing to do to check in.

There's a quiet knock at the door. "Mr. Maxwell?"

"Yes?"

It's my secretary, Miss Dawning. Her expression is slightly hesitant, the wrinkles around her eyes even deeper than normal.

"There's someone here to see you. She doesn't have an appointment, but I told her I'd see if—"

"Who is it?"

"Madelyn Cunnigham."

"Of course. Send her in."

"Oh!" My secretary blinks. No doubt surprised. I typically hate unscheduled meetings and simply decline. "Of course, Mr. Maxwell. Right away." As she closes my office door, she holds the lone pearl dangling from her gold necklace over her white blouse, an amused look on her face.

A moment later, my secretary leads Maddie into my

office. Maddie flashes her that same bright smile she used when she was crossing the street, then looks at me. The smile gets smaller...and hotter. Pink spreads across her cheeks. Her doe eyes take on a sensual heat.

This isn't how she looked at the doorman.

I can't help the pull of an asymmetrical grin at the sight of her reaction.

"Hello, Maddie." The scent of her perfume has already spread lightly across the office. "I'm surprised to see you here during business hours." The camera didn't do her justice. She's even more beautiful in person. My grip tightens on the desk as she makes her way in.

She laughs, a little nervously. "I just finished some errands, and you're my next stop. Do you have a few minutes?"

I gesture to the chair across from my desk. "For you?" I pause, allowing a moment to pass while our eyes lock. "Of course I have time."

Maddie blushes a deeper red and moves across the office. The modern lines of my office furniture are hard and sharp, there's a coldness in its simplicity, and then there's her. Warmth and beauty and femininity. I settle back into my chair and she takes her seat, balancing her purse neatly on her lap. I don't know which I like more—Maddie in a bodysuit or Maddie in this classic dress.

She smiles hesitantly across the desk at me. "So...I have some bad news."

My blood runs cold and I despise the worrying tone she has. If she were mine, she wouldn't have to worry about a damn thing. "What kind of bad news?" I keep my voice calm, but I'm anything but. I don't want to hear that she has bad news—if someone's done something to her, like her ex-fiancé, it needs to be fixed immediately. My palms itch and it takes great effort not to let on every scenario that runs through the back of my mind.

"I may have...well, I *did* break a window in the apartment. Yesterday." The corners of Maddie's mouth turns down. "It was an accident. My phone completely slipped out of my hand, and I never expected..." She takes a deep and steadying inhale. "I know repairs like that get added to the rent, so I've visited two different places to see if I could figure out a way to afford it, but—"

"Let me guess. It was the picture window?"

Maddie bites her lip and gives me an embarrassed nod. Fuck, my cock is so hard precum leaks from the seam. If I could have created a storyline for us to play, this would be fucking perfect.

"None of the companies would agree to work on a project like that. Too complicated with the large sheet of glass. Not worth the trouble," I tell her. There's no way in hell she's going to find someone to come and fix that window. I have my contacts though; it's not a problem in the least.

"That's exactly what I found out." Maddie leans forward,

her lips parted, clearly trying to decide what to say next. "I didn't want to...I don't want you to think I'm making any assumptions about—"

"What kind of man I am?"

Her eyes snap to mine. "I don't see anything wrong with... with making more deals, if it's two consenting adults, and I..."

She pauses for so long that I lean in, too. If it wasn't for the desk between us, I'd have her in my lap already.

"You were thinking about the last deal we made, weren't you?"

"I was," she admits in a soft voice. "I was thinking about it. I...I liked it."

"I told you I'd make it good for you."

"And you did." She looks down and away, collecting herself. "So I wondered if you'd be willing to make another arrangement with me." The vulnerability in her tone is a temptress herself.

I know what I should say to her. I know that I should keep my focus where it belongs—on the deals I'm trying to make and the goals I'm trying to reach. I shouldn't take advantage of her situation.

I just can't do that. I can't be that man. I want her too much.

"I'd be happy to do that, if it's what you would like to do."

Her eyes widen, the heat in her gaze simmering. "You would?"

"I wanted you the first time we came to an agreement," I say, hoping to hell I don't sound as if I'm completely smitten with her. "I still do."

"Okay." Maddie glances over my desk. "Is this—"

"Not here. I'll come up to your apartment when I'm finished for the day." As soon as the words are out of my mouth, I regret them. Why the hell *not* here? I'd like to fuck her on my desk. Fucking hell, I can only imagine how hot she'd look. I'd like to see her all spread out over my paperwork. But that would be a decision based on my cock, and I didn't get where I am by constantly leading with my dick.

She nods in agreement and asks politely, "Is there anything I can do in the meantime?"

"I'll make the calls and the repair crew should be here within the next hour or two. The company I work with never makes me wait more than an hour, so they should be done by the time I wrap up for the day."

"Wow." Maddie looks me up and down. "I thought it would take at least a week or…I don't know, even longer."

"And leave you with a broken window?" I shake my head. "Next time there's anything broken, call me as soon as it happens. Don't let it sit overnight."

"I didn't cut myself or anything," Maddie says. "It's more like a spiderweb."

"As soon as it happens," I insist, lowering my voice.

A sexy shiver runs through her and it's addictive. "Okay," she whispers, then clears her throat. "Okay, Mr. Maxwell. I'll do that."

I get up from my chair and help her out of hers, ignoring the intense urge to slide my hand up under her dress to see how wet she is. I already know how much this turns her on.

It'll be torture for me and probably for her, too, but I need to reinforce my self-control.

I guide Maddie to the door with my hand on the small of her back. She looks up at me and murmurs a quick *thank you,* and then I watch her walk away, ignoring the prying look from Miss Dawning.

CHAPTER 4

MADDIE

It happened unbelievably fast—the window's fixed and the crew is already gone. They were the most efficient team I could have imagined. I barely had time to go through two applications in that time they were here.

They weren't like the repair places I visited earlier. In those places, the men behind the counter shook their heads even as I was telling them the problem. I could already tell they wouldn't take the job.

This crew came in as a team, moved fast, and had the big pane of glass out of the frame and replaced in less than an hour.

For them it was a quick fix.

For me it was the longest day of my life. I made a compromise and it's one I'm trying not to think about as I pace behind my sofa and stare at the blue door to my apartment. Waiting for the knock. Waiting for the payment to be made. I close my eyes, take a deep breath in, and breathe out slowly.

All I want is for Graham to get here.

I realize that a second deal with him is past the point where I can explain it away through sheer desperation, but he smelled too damn good. Afterall, damages are probably covered by renters' insurance...maybe? I'm sure there could have been another way. I didn't want it any other way, though. He looked at me with those gorgeous blue eyes, and I wanted to feel his hands on me again. I wanted to give him something, too.

I hadn't actually meant to make another arrangement with him, though. What I'd meant to do was go to his office, confess what had happened, then ask him for the name of someone who could fix the window. I'd have called myself and asked about a payment plan, something to make it affordable. Or given the information to insurance. I'm sure there is some other way to handle an accident like that. I'm almost one hundred percent certain.

And then he'd been there, sitting behind his desk, so handsome and charming and a little bit, what felt like, protective and flirtatious. I couldn't help myself.

The clock behind me in the kitchen ticks.

I can hear it in the quiet of the apartment. I'm standing in a spacious entryway, which happens to be the first—no, *second*—place I ever saw Graham. An open archway leads into the kitchen. The entryway leads into the wide living room with the big windows I've loved since I moved in. My bedroom and bathroom are off to the left. My ex's office is to the right of the living room. I wanted to make it a guest bedroom, but now it's just...empty. Empty and luxurious, with crown molding and a calming paint job and enough room for my cousin, *if* she'd agree to live with me.

Graham's going to be here any minute. Standing right where he was before.

I take deep breaths and pretend to be calm about it. There's nothing out of place in the entire apartment. I've already cleaned everything there is to clean. I've prepared myself as best as I can as well.

A text pops up on my phone and I'm more than grateful for the distraction. It's from Kenzie.

Kenzie: Hey, Maddie, I'm sorry about the phone call the other day

Maddie: It's okay! Are things any better?

Kenzie: Not really, but I don't want to fight with you or take out my frustrations on you. I love you.

Maddie: I love you too and we're not fighting. Call me later if you want?

Kenzie: I will.

I don't think she will call. Her texts make me believe she might be in a worse financial situation than before, and she feels like she needs to be on good terms with me just in case.

If only she knew the bad luck I've been having. A broken window doesn't help anybody who's short on cash.

I'll be all right. I'll get back on my feet. Until then…I glance back at the door, willing there to be a knock on the other side.

The only thing that worries me is how much I've been thinking about Graham, what we did together, and the way I feel when he's touching me.

After my last two exes, I don't need to fall head over heels with a man, especially one with so much more than what I have. More power and an imbalance…it's exactly what got me into this problem in the first place. I fell in love with a man who was far more wealthy and powerful than me. I did everything he wanted to feel safe and because I loved him. I'm not saying I'm in love with Graham, but I am saying it's something I need to be aware of.

Nothing has felt as new and exciting as being near Graham, but how can I trust that feeling when it's led me to disaster more than once?

I have to be careful. The romantic in me needs to die. This is just sex. It's practically business…an arrangement sealed with a kiss.

Shaking off the hesitation, I go to the bedroom and plug my phone in on the side table, doing my best to keep thoughts of Kenzie and my job search and my past out of my head. Today is about the present. Today is about giving Graham what I owe for the broken window.

Another wave of desire runs through me, and I wonder if I should wait for him naked on the sofa or if he would want me to strip for him again. He seemed to really like that. The memory brings a heat through my chest.

That probably shouldn't be so hot to think about, but I already have to press my thighs together to keep myself from stripping out of my clothes and having some private time in the bedroom. Graham seemed to like my dress when he saw it earlier, so I decide to keep it on.

I peek down at the phone to make sure it's charging and that's when I notice the time: five o'clock.

It's officially the end of the workday.

I hover in the living room, waiting. I want to stand right next to the door and pull it open the second I hear footsteps, but that would make me look...

I don't know how it would make me look. Too eager? Too into him? I've never been very good at playing. I've always worn my heart on my sleeve, and no amount of forbidden sex with the man who owns my building is going to change something that's right at the center of my personality.

Sometimes I wish I could be cool and collected and keep my cards close to my chest, but that's never been me.

The knock at the door is loud and confident, and I know before I get to the peephole that it's him. Graham stands on the other side of the glass. Even with this strange fisheye view, he's the most handsome man I've ever seen. His suit is sharp, his tie undone and laying over his collar. It's sexy as fuck.

I square my shoulders, lift my chin, and open the door.

The man who stands in the hall is every bit as tall and beautiful as he was before, but not as reserved. He has a darker look in his eyes. Before, he didn't let me see the hunger in them until he was sitting down with me. Now it's apparent, as if he's not even trying to hide it.

"Madelyn," he says, his voice low, a certain strain in it like he's been holding in how much he wants this all day. Maybe even all week.

"Graham," I respond, opening the door wider and waving him in.

As soon as the door closes behind him, he takes my chin in his hand, tilts my face up to his, and looks into my eyes.

"Did any of the repairmen bother you?"

"Bother me?" I let out a giggle. "No, of course not. They were perfectly professional."

"Good. Is the window fixed?"

"It's in one piece again. They were very fast about it. You would've been impressed."

"I doubt anything could impress me as much as you in this dress." His eyes drop down over my body, and I'm *so* glad I didn't change. "I think that's what you owe me for the window."

"My dress?" His hand on my face is gentle, but I can feel the strength behind it. "You want me to give you my dress?"

"I want you to give me your body in that dress," he says, then leans in and kisses me.

It's a hard kiss, harder than I thought it would be, and Graham lets out a relieved sound like the most frustrating part of his day is that he wasn't already here to kiss me and fuck me and...whatever else he has planned.

When he pulls back, I'm short of breath from the intensity of the kiss. "I can give that to you. Just...just tell me where."

With a sexy grin, Graham guides me into the kitchen. It's bright and spacious and clean. I'd expected him to take me to the bedroom, but instead he lifts me up and puts me on the countertop I wiped down three times today. With his hands on my waist, he leans down to drag his teeth over the side of my neck. Shivers run down my body and my nipples harden. Graham inhales deeply, and his lips brush over the same spot before his hands slide down and he spreads my thighs.

It makes my dress hitch up and he pushes it higher, almost to my waist, exposing the matching fabric of my panties. I give myself to him without hesitation. I want this more than he could possibly know.

"Did you wear these for me?" He asks in a low tone, gliding a finger underneath the lace waistband and dragging it away from my skin. Graham lets the panties fall back into place, then pulls them away again, letting cool air come into contact with the dampness between my thighs.

"Yes," I answer, dizzy from the way he touches me ever so

slightly with his knuckle.

"How hard did you try to get the window fixed?" he muses, pulling the panties a little farther out from my skin and letting his fingers move toward my clit. I spread my thighs a little more. "Or did you plan to come to me the whole time?"

His fingers dip down, his knuckles making faint contact with my clit, and I moan out loud.

"No, I tried," I tell him, my face hot, the space between my thighs even hotter.

His fingertips stroke fully against my clit. "I could've told you that you'd never find anyone to fix this window. And then you walked into my office and made an offer. You knew I'd take you up on it, didn't you?" he questions, and there's an edge to his tone.

"I hoped you would," I answer honestly, my eyes caught in his gaze like a hunter to the prey.

"You should *know* I want you," he says as if it's a command. I almost tell him yes Sir. So close to being weak for him and putty in his hands.

"I want you, too." I tell him, although it's barely spoken under my chaotic breath.

"Are you in need Madelyn?" he questions, and my cheeks go hot.

I need his fingertips on me more than life.

"I want more from you this time," he says in a gravelly voice before I can answer. "I don't just want to make it good.

I want to see how good it is by the expression on your face. Look at me."

I look into his pale blue eyes, overwhelmed by his hand moving under the lace of my panties. He stops, and I freeze. "Did I do something wrong?"

His eyes glint. "No, kitten, you didn't. I just need to get these out of the way."

He strips my panties off slowly, bringing them gently over my thighs, and crushes them into a ball in his fist. The rip of the lace tearing is audible, and it makes my bottom lip drop.

"You wanted this, didn't you? Your panties are already wet."

I spread my legs a little more for him, feeling reckless at the way he called me *needy*.

Yes. I want to be your little whore, I think, but I don't tell him that. I'm too afraid to.

"That's it." His fingers return to my core, and he pushes two of them inside me, letting out a hiss when they sink in easily.

"I want to watch you come for me," he says as my pleasure climbs with every thrust of his fingers. He moves his thumb in relentless little circles over my clit, the pleasure building and building, his blue eyes locked on mine. There's nothing to do but keep my thighs open for him and come, clenching on his fingers. My toes curl as my body heats and I get closer and closer.

"Fuck, Graham," I call out his name as I reach my climax all too easily.

His face is flushed, his eyes dark, and he leans between my legs and unzips his pants.

This is the sight I didn't get to see before. He was bent over me from behind, and I didn't get to see how he looks when he wants from me this badly.

When he wants *me* this badly. It's a heady feeling, to know a man like him wants me.

I feel like I might lose my mind from wanting him, so I wrap my legs around his waist as he lines himself up and pushes in. He's much thicker than his fingers and I gasp at the stretch. My head falls back in pure bliss, but his hand cradles the back of my head and instantly his lips are on mine.

Graham isn't rough, but he doesn't hold back, either. He moves against me with smooth, powerful thrusts, his hands bracing me where he wants me.

"Fuck," he says. His voice is low, and it does nothing but make me hotter for him.

Graham kisses me with passion, his hands roam my body, and the sensations are all too much at once, and yet at the same time, not enough. He takes control of my mouth completely, tasting me deeply, and I taste him back as his hips work faster and deeper, pushing in until he bottoms out. Desire screams through my veins with a scorching heat and I can't get enough. He tenses, his body going still, and then he wraps his hands around my ass and grinds me against him while he comes. My orgasm hits right before his, turning my mind to sheer pleasure.

I'm not sure exactly what happens. He says something to me, but none of the words make much sense. He lifts me into his arms and takes me through the apartment to my bedroom.

He leaves me for the bathroom, and I catch my breath and slip on a nightie. The faucet runs in the bathroom, and I attempt to figure out what to say, but my mind is blank.

I have to say something about the window. I have to thank him...and maybe tell him I like our arrangement more than I thought I would. But I don't want it to seem like I want money from him. The words stay scrambled in my mind as he comes back out, gorgeous muscles on full display. It's then that a phone goes off from the living room.

"Wait here a moment," he tells me before giving me a searing kiss. I lie down under the sheets sated and exhausted, just barely able to hear him answer the phone. I try to think about what to say and how to handle this in a way where he knows I could be interested in more.

He comes into the room, a hand over his phone and tells me he'll be right back. But he's gone before I can answer. The apartment door opens and closes, and I'm left in bed alone.

It doesn't take long for me to rest my eyes and somehow, I drift into sleep.

When I wake up in the morning, it's quiet in my apartment. Thoughts that the night before was only a dream come to mind, but the soreness between my thighs shuts that down immediately. The only sound is the heating and cooling system and its whisper of air. If I lie very still, I can just make out the hum of the fridge in the kitchen. Eight stories below, the city is already awake. Cars honk in the traffic. Breaks squeal. I'll be out there soon, looking for a job.

For now, I roll over onto my back and stretch. I feel good. Well rested. Well fucked, if I'm being honest. I slept deeply all night and didn't wake up worried about anything.

Sunlight streams through the window, and it's like Graham was never there.

I swallow thickly, realizing he never came back. I force myself to shut down all emotion that creeps in and instead concern myself with the task of getting a job so I never have to approach Graham for another arrangement again.

CHAPTER 5

GRAHAM

Usually, when I get together with one of my friends—*if* I have time to get together with a friend—it's business that distracts me. There's never a moment there isn't something to do. Someone is always waiting, the emails never stop. There are fires and problems everywhere and every day.

I know I shouldn't let my work life get in the way of relationships, but if I don't do it, no one else will. And more importantly, everything I've spent years working my ass off for could unravel.

My friend Brian, with short brownish red hair and a five o'clock shadow, sits across from me at a sports bar that rides the line between upscale and pretentious. The TVs boast the football game and I know Brian has a couple hundred riding on it.

On the next run, when Brian settles into our booth with his hand curled around his beer and his eyes focused on the play, I take out my phone. I tap the screen and scroll through the emails that have come through. But I'm also checking for something else.

Any messages from Maddie.

She hasn't sent one, but I have half a message typed out.

No pressure, but I was thinking...

It's a ridiculous way to start a text. I delete it and try again.

The apartment building is nice, but there are other places we could go, if you were interested in...

That's a smooth way to ask a woman out. By reminding her that other places exist. I delete it all again with frustration that Brian picks up on. His gaze drops to my phone and then back to the flat screen TV. I'm sure he assumes it's just business. Heat scorches the back of my neck. In a way, that's what it is. *But I want more.*

I clear my throat and take a swig of my beer.

I want to ask her out. That's the whole point of writing and rewriting the text. I just don't know how, given the way things started between us.

I'm willing to accept responsibility for that. I just don't know how to fucking fix it.

"Always the emails, right?" Brian smiles at me, his eyes crinkling. He's the same way. We keep tabs on our money at all hours of the day. "They never stop."

I swipe into my email app just so I'm not a total liar. "Yeah. That's how it goes." He must sense something off because his eyes narrow, and even though the next play starts, he doesn't give the TV his attention.

"What's new with you?"

"More acquisitions," I tell him, that burning feeling at the back of my neck comes back at the thought of my most recent *acquisition*. "Getting into stocks and hedge funds as well."

"Sounds boring," he states and then takes a large gulp of beer.

I laugh at that—can't help it. Brian works on Wall Street, like he always planned to. He came from money, but not the kind the two of us are making now. He always wanted to get to that next level, and Brian's done it without leaving a single thing behind, unlike me.

I guess I haven't left Brian behind, which is saying something. We've been friends since grade school. His parents are proud of him. They've said they're proud of me, too, and they've always been kind, but I don't see them as family.

Brian and I watch the game until a commercial break comes on. He orders chips and salsa, then looks at me across the table.

"You should come to the Berkshires with us this winter," he suggests.

I've been there before. They have a nice place, but it's a

little too family-oriented for my liking. It makes sense for Brian to want to go, though. He's married, and before too long, they'll only want places that are family-oriented.

I tend to my drink and ignore how that makes me feel cold.

Not the Berkshires in the winter, but Brian and his wife—all my friends and their wives—becoming *families*, with me on the outside.

I've never wanted a family or a *replacement* family. Not since my parents died. Families are a limited-time thing. They always fall apart and it fucking hurts when they do.

The waitress comes back and puts the chips and salsa between us. Brian dips a chip into the salsa and looks at me, eyebrows raised.

"We'll see," I hedge.

Brian scoffs. "What else are you going to do? Sit in your fancy penthouse alone?"

I've never thought much about being alone in my penthouse on Christmas. It's another day. There's nowhere to go on Christmas, and the more my friends pair off, the less I feel welcome going to their places on holidays. Who wants a lonely third wheel on Christmas morning? I won't be someone's burden.

Thoughts of what Maddie will do this winter come to mind and I find myself curious.

My life hasn't been empty. It's been full of goals to meet and money to make and projects to close. Then Maddie came into it, and now I can't see anything *but* how empty all of it is. A great big penthouse. Me on my phone. Snow falling outside. Christmas, and no one to open presents in the light of the tree.

I glance back at my phone and think about texting her.

I could...offer to tend to her needs. Take care of her. If she wants.

I still don't know how to say it though. How to present the offer in an acceptable manner. Especially given it will be in writing.

Half of what I want to say should never be written in black and white.

Even if I want her in my penthouse on Christmas. Fuck I could just imagine unwrapping her lingerie as if she's my personal gift.

I glance down at the black text and my thumb taps aimlessly.

I don't want to sound like I'm offering money for her company, or anything of that manner. Like I'm paying her for companionship.

Although if money is what she would want, I'd give it to her. A *Pretty Woman*-esque arrangement.

"What's going on with you?" Brian asks, his tone careful. "You're quiet."

I watch the game on the TV, purposely not looking at my phone, and try to figure out what the hell to tell my oldest friend in the world. If I told him it was nothing and to drop it, Brian probably would. But then I'd be exactly where I was when I came into this bar.

"I'm thinking about asking a woman out." I blurt it out without looking at him.

Brian lets out a low whistle. "Look at you. This girl must really be something for you to keep checking your phone like that and looking like a nervous school kid."

Normally, I'd deny the hell out of it. I *always* check my phone. That's not new. And if I look nervous, that's because I have other things to be nervous about.

But this is Brian and he's asking, and for once it seems important to tell the truth. Because I am all too aware I need help. Afterall, he landed a wife. He has to know something about this arena that I don't.

"It's just...someone. I met under odd circumstances."

"What kind of—"

"Don't ask about the circumstances." I cut him off, a little harsher than intended and hold his gaze a moment too long.

"Okay?" He raises his eyebrows. "And you want to ask her on a date?"

"I would like to, yes. And maybe more. I don't know."

"More?"

Frustration gets the best of me as I run my hand through my hair. "I'm telling you, it's ridiculous. I can't stop thinking about her."

"I'm not asking about the circumstances," Brian says after a minute. "But...is that what's making it tough for you to ask her out?"

"Yeah. You could say that."

"Maybe you just have to forget about the circumstances, then."

I can't. A huff of a sarcastic laugh leaves me. There's no way in hell I could forget what happened...it's burned into my memory.

"Things can always change." Brian eats another chip with salsa. He pushes the basket toward me. "I think it's best if you take matters into your own hands. Just let her know what you want. It's like an offer," he suggests and motions with his hand as if I should know how to make an offer.

It takes great effort to breathe evenly and consider a response other than *I've done that. I literally took Maddie into my own hands, and now there's always going to be some kind of tension between us.*

"And if I already have...made an offer, that is? If it's too late to change the way she sees me?"

I don't even know *how* she sees me. All this is based on my own assumptions and the unwanted anxious emotions I can't seem to shake off.

"What kind of an offer?" he questions, and I shake my head once. He readjusts in his seat. "You made an ass out of yourself or something?"

"Don't ask."

"You're not giving me much here," he mutters, and then a foul is made on the screen and the corner of the bar erupts with outrage that distracts us both for a moment.

It settles quickly enough.

He finally says, "Just talk to her. What's the worst that could happen?"

That I lose her, obviously. The chance to have her fill this emptiness that's been glaringly apparent slips through my fingers.

When the chips are gone and the game is over, I haven't decided what to send in a text. All I've decided is to wait until the next time rent is due.

CHAPTER 6

MADDIE

My friend Suzette breezes into the café with a wide, bright smile on her face. It's the kind that says she has good news, and God, I hope she does.

Even if it means I won't have to go to Graham and ask for help anymore. Thoughts of him make my thighs tighten and a shiver of want runs down my shoulders. He has a little spell on me. I'm certain it's because of my broken heart and hopeless ways with men. I need to shake it off. I need to shake *him* off.

I ignore the sharp feeling of regret at that thought. After Kevin, I've learned my lesson. But I can't help it if I loved having Graham in my kitchen. It felt forbidden but familiar at the same time, like something we both needed. Almost like the broken window didn't matter at all.

I loved every second of it, but it can only be a moment of my life. And now it's time for me to move on.

Pushing those thoughts from my head, I stand up and wave at Suzette, returning her smile with the biggest one I can. "Hi! How are you?"

With wide steps that cause her red-soled heels to click on the floor, she comes over and gives me a quick hug, smelling like the fresh air outside and her hairspray. "How are *you*? You look like you're doing so much better!" Her jet-black hair with a blunt bob and bangs pairs perfectly with her sharply cut dress that hugs her curves. She looks expensive, mostly because everything she touches is expensive. Her hug is nothing but warmth and compassion. Just like always. I might have bad luck with men, but with my friend group, it's always been wonderful. All of them are married and they don't have quite as much time as they used to, but still, I'm grateful I have good friends in my life.

We take our seats at the table and the barista brings us our coffees as we make small talk. It's easy and Suzette updates me on her new place and what Julia and Kat have been up to. Suzette sips her coffee with an appreciative grin. The café is bustling at this hour of the morning, and the sound of other people chatting does something great for my nerves. At the counter, a guy is flirting with the barista, and she's flirting back. Maybe I should've spent more time meeting men in cafés instead of…well in dire circumstances.

But then I wouldn't be where I am now. Granted, being jobless and late on rent isn't great. I can't argue with the other parts of my life having abundance, though, and I'm grateful for that.

"Have you find your dream job yet?" Suzette asks when a moment of quiet passes.

"Not exactly, but soon." I hold up crossed fingers. "I've been applying for jobs like my life depends on it."

I'm not kidding. I must've applied for forty jobs since Graham left my kitchen last week. I've written and rewritten my resume twice as many times, trying to frame my charity board experience in the best light possible. It's really too bad I can't figure out a way to fit in *problem-solving by getting the hot rich man who owns my building to float me the rent*, because that feels like a real achievement as well.

"Like your life depends on it," Suzette shakes her head as she repeats what I've said, raising her eyebrows. "Doesn't money always feel like that? I really think you should have called me sooner."

I make a face at her. "I didn't want to." In truth, my friends are much better off in life than I am. But I'd never want to burden them. Even venting to Suzette felt wrong. I didn't want her to take it the wrong way. A bottle of pinot will really open me up though.

"Why not?"

"Because I was such a mess before Kevin, and you had to... you know. You were there for all of that."

"I was *glad* to be there for all of that," she says firmly. "That's what being friends is for. Being there for one another even when things get shitty."

I can feel it, all over again, how heartbroken, confused, and angry I was. That was a breakup that seemed to last forever. I would wake up in the morning and swear I was over it, and by evening I'd be calling Suzette again to vent just so I could hold back tears.

I hadn't wanted to tell her what happened with Kevin, too, because in some ways it felt like *my* failure.

I don't think that anymore.

It doesn't make it easier to let other people see me when I'm down...again.

So I'm not going to be down. Not about this, even if what was supposed to be a simple transaction is turning out to be more complicated than I thought, at least in the feelings department. I remind myself again that I can't make assumptions about what Graham feels—I *won't* make assumptions. That'll get you into trouble faster than your fiancé can say *I'm leaving.*

"You're right." I take a drink of my hot coffee, savoring the warmth and the flavor. That's a good reminder that no matter how hard things get, there are still parts of life that are *wonderful.* Like coffee with hazelnut flavoring. "But we're here now."

"Next time, just call me," she insists in a serious voice, but cracks a smile. "Because I have good news."

"What kind of news?"

"Good news for you, silly." She twists in her seat and looks through her purse, then pulls out a business card. Suzette slides it across the table like it's worth a million bucks.

I take the card and turn it over. It's the classy kind of business card—thick paper, smooth ink. This isn't the cheap kind you can get at any office supply store.

The name on the front reads Michael Davies, CEO.

"What is this? I mean, *who* is this?"

Suzette smiles, pleased with herself. "I asked around, and it turns out a friend of a friend has a close friend whose company consults with nonprofits."

I tip the card one way, then another, watching the light move on the embossed letters. "Consultation?"

"It's right up your alley, Maddie."

The name seems to ring a bell and then I read the website on the back and the tagline. "Wait, I applied for this place." I nearly gasp as I the realization dawns of me. The company name looks familiar when it didn't only moments before. "Only I applied to work in filing, not as anyone's assistant or consultant."

"Well, the CEO needs an assistant with a consultation background, and you have tons of experience."

"I don't, though. I've never worked as a consultant."

"On the other side, I meant. You were on all those boards. And it's not like that's all you've ever done. You had jobs on boards before and always made it work. You know the ins and outs, and you have recent insight into costs and strategy. Don't sell yourself short."

I stare at her across the table. "You spun my board experience into a lead?" My heart pounds; I was on boards but it's not like I was making the executive decisions. I have insight yes, but I wasn't in charge of any major decisions.

"You can lean in this direction. Don't undersell yourself."

"I just don't want to oversell myself," I tell her.

A knot in my chest releases. I hadn't known how much stress I was actually under until Suzette handed me this card.

"That's impossible to do, Maddie. You have so much worth to provide. And they need it. Truly, this will be a match made in heaven."

I let her words sink in and think back to all the strategy meetings. I did have a lot of success in that department, and more than that, I loved doing it. "It's good to hear you say that, because I've felt like a total fraud lately."

"Don't." She waves a hand in the air. "The last thing you are is a fraud. And if Michael thought so, he wouldn't have given me a card. All you need to do is call and set up the interview."

"You have no idea how good that sounds."

"It's not going to be good, it's going to be *great*." Suzette beams at me. "And, honestly, I don't think you'd be an assistant very long. Once he sees how good you are at fundraising, he'll have no choice but to put you in charge of a team."

"A *team*?"

"They have a whole department just for gifts and philanthropy. You'll get your foot in the door, and it'll be like that." She snaps her fingers.

"Oh, wow." I take a few deep breaths, feeling lighter and hopeful once again. "That's...thank you. I was starting to lose hope a bit on the job front. Having a rich fiancé isn't impressive on a résumé."

"Well..." Suzette gives me a meaningful look. "You don't have a rich fiancé now." She glances around the café as if we might be overheard. "You know what? Michael's building isn't far from here. Why don't we walk over and see it?"

We take our coffees and go. I'm equally nervous and excited. Suzette's confident enough for the both of us about this new job. I fall for her enthusiasm hook, line, and sinker. It only takes a block or two for excitement to win.

"So." Suzette tosses her empty cup into a garbage bin. "What had you so excited before I gave you the best job lead ever?"

"Oh, it's probably not...it's nothing, really."

"Did you meet someone?" she guesses. Suzette is sharp as a whip.

My face gets hot. The truth is that part of me wants to tell everybody I meet about Graham, but the other part wants to keep him a secret. That way, what we have together only belongs to me. Well that and the fact that I exchanged sex for rent also stays a secret.

"Maddie!" Suzette nudges my elbow with hers, and for a second I fear she can read my mind. "I can see you blushing. Did you meet a guy? No, no...tell me *where* you met a guy. I can tell you have a crush."

I swallow thickly, holding onto my paper coffee cup with both hands. "You can't say anything."

Her eyebrows go up. "A secret boyfriend?" I can tell she wants to laugh, and I let out a long breath.

"He's not my *boyfriend*." I glance around us, but there's nobody even close to recognizable on the street. The city block looks vibrant in the sun. "He's just...someone I met."

"Blind date?"

"Actually..." I steel myself to tell her the truth; my heart beats faster. "I met him in an elevator"—she eyes me, waiting for more details—"and I first saw him when I was still with Kevin."

Her mouth drops open. "*Madelyn*." She whispers my name, and it takes everything in me not to respond *yes, Mother.*

"I didn't find out until after Kevin left that he owns the building."

"And you're *dating*?" she drags out the word as if it's unbelievable. Which it is because we are not dating.

"Shh!" I look around again, but the only people in sight don't seem to have noticed. "And no. We're not dating."

"What *is* going on, then? I know you, and I know something is going on. I have to know!"

My heart beats hard as I question whether or not to tell her. With my nerves racing and her wide eyes boring into me with desperation, I know I have to tell her. Besides, Suzette would never judge me. She's been married, divorced, and involved in an office scandal with her boss. All the while, I've been there for her. I swallow down my fears knowing out of all the people in the world, she might get what I'm feeling. The good and the bad.

"I needed some help with the rent." Now that the moment is here, I don't know how to describe it in a way that's not going to make it seem...immoral. "So I asked, and he offered me an...arrangement."

Her eyes brighten. Her cheeks turn a bright pink and her voice raises in octave. "Like...a sexy arrangement?"

"You wouldn't believe how sexy it is."

Suzette tips her head back and stares at the sky in disbelief. Then she picks it back up and looks at me. "Maddie, that's—"

"Wrong. I know. I shouldn't sleep with anyone to pay the rent, much less—"

"That's *hot*." She corrects, stopping in her tracks and waiting for me to look her in the eyes.

"—a man who happens to...what?" It takes me a moment

to realize what she's said.

"That's hot. And adventurous. I don't think I'd have been brave enough to take him up on it. Was it in his office?"

"My place."

"So now your rent's covered for the year?"

"The month," I say quickly. "It's not supposed to be anything long-term. A one-time deal...that turned into a two-time thing." I start to explain but then slam my lips shut.

Suzette immediately looks skeptical. "Yeah, right. I bet he fell for you already. There will be a third time," she states matter of factly, taking a sip of her coffee. We continue walking down the sidewalks of Manhattan.

I think of Graham standing at the door of my apartment, his eyes dark, desire clear on his face. At the time, I wouldn't have said it was love, and I probably still wouldn't, because...

Because that would be getting my hopes up for nothing. What I have with Graham was never meant to be about a relationship. If he'd wanted that, I'm sure he would've said as much.

And I'm not falling for him, either. Fantasizing about different excuses to get him to my apartment again doesn't mean love, it means that he's so sexy I can't breathe, I like the feel of his hands on my body, and I want to know more about him.

Not that I'm in *love.*

"I'd put money down that there's going to be a third

arrangement." She mocks the way I said it and I can't help but blush.

"I don't think so." I hold my head high. "It was just a... business deal."

"Then why do you have that look on your face?" she asks me softly and I wish I wasn't so easy to read.

Suzette's known me long enough to know that I love falling in love. Sex and love are hard for me to separate. I think. I don't know. It's just the way I am. I love the rush at the beginning and the giddy feelings whenever you get to see the other person and how it seems impossible to spend even five minutes apart.

She *also* knows how devastating it can be when it all falls apart. She was there through the last major breakup I had before I met Kevin, and she stuck by me through the ups and downs without ever saying *I told you so.*

"It's just about having fun?" she questions softly.

"It's about paying the rent." I glance over at her, and the corners of her mouth are turned up. "And...yes. It's fun."

"As long as you're happy."

"I am happy enough to leave that behind. And now that I have this lead, I'm sure I'll be *very* happy."

We reach the building where Michael Davies' company is housed. It's a sky-high, gleaming tower that says *this is a business doing important things in the world.*

It reminds me of my apartment building. Graham's

building isn't quite as tall as this one, but it has a vibe to it that says *important people live here, and they love it. You would love to live here, too.*

I try to blink away the thoughts of him as Suzette rambles on about the company.

"The company's housed on the tenth floor, so you'll have a view when you're at work." Suzette counts the floors with a fingertip in the air, then points. "That'll be nice, right?"

"Really nice." Even if all I can think about is the view from my very own apartment. Every time I look at the windows, I think of Graham, and the way he feels when he's inside me. I wonder if I'll think of him the same way if I get this job and head to the office every morning. I wonder if I could even stay in that apartment...or if I should.

Suzette and I stare up at the building together, taking it all in. She's right. This is going to be it. This is going to be the job that puts me on the path to a life I want.

She would know. I watched Suzette accidentally fall into love, too. It was a sizzling scandal and I freaking loved that for her. Miss prim and proper and all business, doing the deed in her boss' office...apparently against the skyscraper window too. She knows a thing or two about unorthodox relations. Years later, it's easy to see how happy she is. Everything turned out just the way it was supposed to for her.

And it's going to turn out that way for me, too.

Hope warms itself in my chest. I've been called naïve

plenty of times in my life. People want me to be more cynical about the world. For some reason, it bothers them that I want to be optimistic. And yes, sometimes I'm not. Sometimes, in the middle of the night, I forget that worrying doesn't help anything.

Action helps. Doing things helps. Meeting handsome men and asking them for help with the rent helps.

There I go again.

A soft laugh from Suzette pulls my attention away from the building and back to her.

"What's so funny?"

"You," she says gently. "I can tell you're thinking about him."

I blush violently and then blatantly lie. "I'm not. I was thinking about how this job could help me get my life back on track. And after *that,* I'm never letting it get off track again."

"That's my girl," Suzette says, and loops her arm through mine. "Call this afternoon to set up an interview. He's waiting for the call."

"Call? Shouldn't I submit a separate application? Send some emails or something?"

She shakes her head. "I told you, I asked around. They're going to be ready for you. Just call, and I'd bet anything you'll be headed in to work on Monday."

Suzette lets out a satisfied sigh. "In the meantime, I want to hear all about this man you're having a torrid affair with."

"A *torrid affair*?" I squeak. "It's not an affair *at all,* Suzette.

We're both very, very single, and I—"

"You needed help with the rent," she says simply.

I needed help with the rent. I nod, and then that unsettling feeling sets in again. "Which is in the past and the whole thing is over," I assure her.

She gives me a skeptical look and I shake my head. "It's done. No more. One-time deal."

She corrects me. "I thought you said it was twice." She peers at me from the corner of her eyes with a smirk.

"Twice and done."

She laughs. "Said no one ever."

CHAPTER 7

GRAHAM

Days go by, and I don't hear from Maddie.

I suppose I didn't expect to hear from her. There's a possibility that by the end of the month she may be in need of another…deal. But likely she'll have found work and given our encounters, she may avoid me.

It's unsettling how much that bothers me and how often I think of her and wonder if when the clock strikes midnight, she'll call. The one thing I'm sure of is that she hasn't moved out. Not that I'm stalking her, but I am aware of her comings and goings from the security cameras.

I check them throughout the day as it stands, so I'm not doing anything out of the ordinary. I'm making sure my residents and my building are both safe and protected.

The third time I check this morning, I find her. I lean back in my seat, holding the cup of black coffee and watch her gorgeous curves sway as she walks. She's so fucking beautiful. How I wasn't obsessed with her for the entirety of her residence here is beyond me.

She heads out of the building at a quarter after eight, wearing a skirt suit that makes me instantly hard at my desk. Maddie leaves with her hair swept back into a bun and her head held high, looking confident and beautiful.

She also carries a powder blue work tote that appears to be large enough for a laptop. The uneasiness that settles at the thought of Madelyn acquiring a job is once again unsettling. It's certainly good for her for a number of reasons to be busy with work and to have an income.

Yet...I find myself at a loss.

I'm far too aware that I don't know what job she got, where she's going, or who she's working for. Clearing my throat, I rock back in my seat, contemplating the possibilities.

I ignore the urge to station myself in the lobby of the building just for the chance to run into her. The things I want to say aren't appropriate for the arrangement we have.

The arrangement we *had*. I don't think, if my instincts are correct and she's now employed, that Maddie needs anything else from me. Look at her, with every single strand of her hair in place, her perfect, pert body, and the spring in her step that says she's got everything under control.

Once she's gone, I turn the monitor off and go back to the tasks at hand, attempting to ignore thoughts of her throughout the day. Coffee comes and goes as do emails. The clock ticks by seemingly slower than it should. Every so often, I imagine Maddie on my desk, her legs spread as they were in her kitchen, and I groan with frustration and have a hardened cock that aches to be inside her again. It's impossible for the hours to tick by without thoughts of her.

Right around five, she comes back from the office the same way, only a little more satisfied, like she made the day hers.

That's what she did. I'm sure of it. I should be glad for her and that's what I tell myself, that I'm glad she has found a way out of the trouble she was in.

A week passes, and then another, and I don't get any other calls about broken windows or being short on rent money that's due any day. I try not to look for her on the cameras, but my little seductress has a routine now. She leaves for work at the same time every day, and most days, she comes home at the same time, unless she goes out with friends. On the weekend, she goes to a yoga class with a slightly older woman who has a ring on her finger and smiles at Maddie like they're close friends.

I hate that I can't let go of thoughts of her unless I'm buried in work. I hate that I feel compelled to initiate a new arrangement with her, but I'm unsure of what exactly it would entail and whether or not she would be interested. I need to ensure the proposal is tempting for her. As tempting as she is to me.

I watch her leave on the screen and then I focus on the business deal sitting in my email, instead of occupying more time with thoughts of a woman who doesn't appear to be thinking of me.

Immediately, I'm agitated and turn from my computer to face the office windows, watching the cars stories below drive past.

Harland Porter is a pain in my ass. He wants to talk about different details every day in no pattern that I can figure out. Every conversation we have makes it tempting as hell to walk away, which only makes me dig my heels in deeper. I can outlast a nervous asshole like Harland Porter. I can grow my empire by one more building. I can have anything I want.

Except Maddie.

To hell with dwelling on her. I'm not going to lose my mind over the fact that she hasn't called, even if it's getting harder to sleep at night. When I do sleep, I dream about her— the way she bent over the furniture, the way she wrapped her legs around me in the kitchen, the way her mouth felt.

The dreams aren't as good as the real thing.

I'm thinking about the real thing *again* near the end of the month, my cock hard and my teeth gritted, when there's a knock at my office door.

Annoyance grows. I'm not to be disturbed and the office

is aware.

Before I can turn around, a feminine and soothing voice says, "Hi, Graham."

It's her.

Adrenaline courses through me and I do everything I can not to show a change in demeanor. As I turn and catch sight of her, I'm forced to slightly readjust myself. A cream-colored lace dress that appears youthful and springish, but also luxurious and even bridal, clings to her as she stands in the threshold. She could be a bride getting married at city hall in one of those ceremonies they feature in the Lifestyle section.

The sight does something to my lungs. I suck the air from them as a stray strand of hair falls in front of her face, and I'm forced to meet her gorgeous gaze.

"Madelyn," I greet her and with her name on my lips, my cock twitches.

She bites her lip, glancing over the office and breaking our heated gaze. "Your secretary wasn't here, so I showed myself in. I hope that's okay."

"Of course. Come in." I gesture to the seat across my desk and take my seat. "Is this about another arrangement?" I ask her and her wide eyes look back at me. I've never felt more on edge as she nods slowly.

"Close the door and lock it." I answer and she obeys. Fuck, I'm harder than I could imagine. It's almost like a game...or like a dream.

Maddie closes the door behind her, her hand hesitates, and then flips the lock. The sound is sinful, and it elicits a raw and desperate need stirring inside of me. Almost like a hunter to a prey, but this prey is coming to me. Fuck, I wish she'd crawl to me.

I almost request it, but I don't want to push my luck.

"Have a seat," I offer and I'm surprised by her response.

She shakes her head, then crosses the room to me in graceful, confident steps. Within seconds she's close enough that I could wrap her in my arms if I wanted. My heart pounds at the doe eyes staring down at me, her heart-shaped lips, and her body in that dress.

"What's this about, Madelyn?" I cross my arms over my chest to keep from touching her. I won't touch her unless she asks. Maybe not until she begs. "It's time to pay the rent again," I state the obvious.

"It is," she murmurs softly. I can practically hear her heart pounding and for a moment I'm taken aback. Speechless. That's not what I thought she'd say at all. Not given she's employed, but perhaps she isn't.

"And you need...an extension? Or...what exactly?"

"I don't want to use you for money," she says and her voice wavers. She swallows thickly and the tension between us heats. "But I liked what we did," she whispers as if it's a confession.

"We can keep doing what we've been doing," I offer, and I

love the very thought of it.

"I thought maybe…it could be…" She swallows thickly, barely able to keep my gaze. "It doesn't have to be about the money," she suggests, and lifts a hand to trace one of the buttons on my shirt.

"I don't want your money, I want you available to me," I tell her, and I've never felt more needy—more greedy—in my fucking life. I want her on her knees sucking my cock. I can already envision those hollowed cheeks. I want her spread on my desk so I can toy with her pretty pink pussy. I want to go home after a long day and fuck her on the edge of her sofa until she screams my name and comes on my cock. "Available whenever I like, and you can have whatever you'd like," I offer, although I second guess how exactly I've presented the deal. I bite my tongue, thinking perhaps a contract should be drawn up. I don't want to get ahead of myself.

"That seems like it could end badly for me." Her doe eyes shine with nothing but vulnerability.

"It could for myself as well," I counter. It could be a disaster, if everything goes to shit because I can't keep my mind off her…and my hands.

And I can't. It's been too long, and I can't stop myself from touching her. I work my fingers through her hair and tip her face up. Maddie blinks like she's on the edge of pleasure already.

"Why did you come here?" I ask her bluntly. As she

attempts to take a half step back, I wrap my hand around her thigh, worried my tone may have been too blunt. "I'm glad you did."

"I just needed a one-week extension, but also…I missed you." I love the way she says she missed me. I have her where I want her, but my head is fogged with nothing but desire. I can barely think straight.

Fuck, my cock aches for her.

"An extension for rent? Because you got a job?"

"Yes. I just need a—"

"I don't care about an extension. I don't want your money Madelyn. I want you to be my little…" I almost say whore. I almost say it, but luckily, she does it for me.

"Your whore?" she questions, and I don't know how she feels about the word.

"My seductress. My…whatever you want to call it. You can be my little whore…if that turns you on." I'm careful with my words, and whatever I'm saying, she seems just as intoxicated by it as I am.

She takes a step forward and I wrap my other hand around her other thigh and turn my chair to face her.

"I'm scared," she admits in a whisper, and I know it's true. It's so fucking obvious.

"We could use a safe word," I suggest quickly and then take a deep steadying breath. "If either of us want to stop."

I take the moment, pulling her toward me and she straddles

me like the good girl she is. Her scent is intoxicating, and her breasts rise and fall with each breath she takes. Maddie tips her head back, making the line of her neck irresistible.

I press a kiss there, then lick over it. "And when it's like this, then a safe word is a good idea."

"Like what?" she questions.

"Intense like this."

She lets out a soft sound when I suck at her neck.

I whisper at the shell of her ear. "When two people who… who like to make deals with each other. When I want to call you my little whore and tell you to crawl to me. When you want me to spoil you. Which, my little seductress, I desperately want to do."

"Like a sugar daddy?" she questions, humor on her lips but her brow is pinched.

"I don't love the name of it. I'd prefer for you to simply be my…my toy, my plaything, my whore—as you suggested. Do you like any of them?"

"I love all of them," she admits, and I press a kiss to her lips. Slow. Savoring every pounding heartbeat between us.

"You could break me so easily and I…I know…" Her eyes beseech me and I know this is what's holding her back. This is what's kept her from me.

"There's a power imbalance I will admit, but a safe word will be helpful. Especially if we are playing this game with boundaries neither of us have pushed before," I suggest. "I've never told anyone to crawl to me," I tell her as I unbuckle my belt. "I've never called anyone a little whore," I admit and sweep my thumb over her bottom lip. "I've never done anything with anyone else like I've done with you."

"I haven't either," she tells me, and I believe her.

"So we need a safe word," I tell her. "That way, we're both safe. We know when to get closer and when to"—I brush a kiss over the curve of her jaw—"and when to back off."

"Mmm. That's a good idea. I agree." She says as her hands find the back of my neck and she lets her head fall back, moving her breasts to my lips. Fuck, I'm hit with a wave of her perfume. My little seductress could be playing me and I wouldn't even fucking care. I'll get everything I want from her and she'll get everything she wants from me.

"Do you really think it's a good idea?"

"Yes. But what word?" she asks in return.

She'll have to take the lead on that one, because I've thought of plenty of things I'd like to say to her, and none of them mean *stop*. They all mean come live in my penthouse. Stop going places where I can't see you. Let me possess you, and I swear I'll take care of everything.

"I intend to fulfill my desires with this arrangement," I tell her. "So I suggest you choose a word you will remember, and one you'll use if you aren't interested in my suggestions."

The tension is thick and hot, and I can see the wheels turning as she thinks of a word. All the while I kiss over the line of her shoulder. The neckline of this dress is demure, office-appropriate, but there's enough skin showing to make me hot as hell. It's like she's inviting me to imagine her body underneath.

Luckily, I don't have to guess. I know. I knead her ass as I wait, and she gasps the sweetest sound.

Gorgeous. Perfect.

I get lost in thinking about what her tits look like and forget she's choosing a safe word for both of us.

"Maybe something like…"

I go back to kissing her neck, and Maddie's entire body responds. She writhes against me, begging to be fucked.

"Think, my little temptress. I need to know that word."

"Temptress," she says and her eyes light with mischievousness. "I like that."

I nuzzle into her neck, commanding her to come up with a word. "What word is going to tell me to stop?" *My temptress.*

"Red," she says.

"Red?" I kiss her just to see if I can taste the word on her lips. I can't. She's much sweeter.

"Red." She breathes. "It's simple and easy."

"Before we start, is there anything you don't want? Anything I've said that you aren't interested in. Crawling, being available anytime…anything?"

"Only when I'm here?" she says although it's a question. "Like I'm available when I'm here, but if I'm out with my friends—"

"When you're here or at preplanned times," I counter.

"If I'm here...in the building...at any time."

"Your pussy is available for me to fuck, as is your ass and your lips."

"My ass...I haven't...I haven't done that before."

"I can go slow. Or is that a 'red' situation?"

She thinks a moment and once again that spark shines in her eyes. "I think I want to try it."

"And if you change your mind, you say red."

She nods. "Right. I can do that."

"I know you can," I tell her and rock my hips, rubbing my cock against her cunt.

"I've never done this before," she tells me again.

"I haven't either but we can take it slow and find the arrangement that works. Right now though, I am more than ready for you to show me how much you want this."

She wastes no time, her hands fly over the buttons of my shirt, popping them open one by one. I don't take the dress off. I want to fuck her in it. She spreads her thighs over mine. I can't get my cock out fast enough, and the second I do, Maddie sinks down on it with a sigh. I keep my hands in her hair and let her work her silk-covered pussy over my shaft.

"Don't fucking tease me." I groan and her eyes spark. "Give me what I want."

"Yes, Sir," she says, and it ignites a deep pleasure inside

of me.

This is everything I want. She is *everything* I've been missing.

Fuck, her cunt is heaven. She rides me with her hands gripped to my shoulders and nothing but pleasure written on her face. Her lips find mine and she moans, and it's everything I need.

She's slow at first and I can tell there's something she's holding back.

Maddie murmurs as she rides me. "I've thought about you every day that I've been in the office. I tried...I don't know." I thrust up and she gasps. "I tried to stay away, thinking it would be better somehow. It's not right to have sex for rent money." Her face is an even deeper red. "I shouldn't have asked you in the first place. But I want it."

"There's not a damn thing wrong with this," I tell her and pump my hips again, forcing a beautiful, tortured sound from her lips. Her dress rides up her hips, showing her bare skin.

She grinds down on me and her eyes go half lidded as her clit rubs against me.

With one hand on her neck and the other on her hip, I help her fuck me harder and deeper. Her blunt nails dig into my shoulders as the pleasure gets the best of her.

She sinks down again and again on my cock, her pussy clenching until I reach between us and give her some contact on her clit. She throws her head back and lets out a soft, sexy moan, her dress hitching up higher on her waist as she comes undone.

I let her ride me, using me to get her off until my own release is too much to hold back. Maddie moves her hips in small circles while I fill her with my own release. My head is full of ways that I could mark her.

Every little sordid thing we can do. And the things I can give her that would tempt her to stay for as long as I want.

I kiss her before my mouth can run away with me. Maddie kisses me back, her body still hot around me. I kiss her slower until her breathing slows down, too, but Maddie stays where she is instead of getting up.

She runs her fingers through my hair. It's a soft touch, intimate like we're actually together, and I let myself indulge in the fantasy for a minute. This is the perfect arrangement.

It doesn't take long for her climb off, and I help her steady herself.

Her eyes find mine and a question lingers there.

"Tell me," I say easily. I'm sure she has questions. Fuck, even I have questions racing in the back of my mind.

"When you say all the time..." she asks. "That I'm available *all* the time."

Yes. All the time. Every second. Every minute. She should be in my office, under my desk, all day until it's time to go back to the penthouse.

"What about it?"

"There will be times when I just want to be alone or I..."

Her hesitation is clear and the one thing I'm not going to do is lose her before it's even begun. "Once a week at least." It's so much less than I want, but it's the only thing I can say to her right now. If I told Maddie the truth, it would go badly. It would be too much for her, and she'd run. Or she'd like it too much, and when it crashed and burned we'd both be taken down with it. "And...if you're in need, I'm the one you'll come to."

"If I'm in need," she repeats quietly.

"If you need to be touched, you call me." I take a hand off her waist and stroke her hair. "If you need to be fucked, you call me. If you wake up in the middle of the night and can't sleep, call me, and I'll make you come until you can."

"What about..." She tilts her head to the side, thinking. "If another window breaks?"

"Don't break your windows on purpose."

"I didn't do it on purpose last time."

"I don't care if it's a broken window or a needy pussy. You call me. Only me. Nobody else."

Her eyes come back to mine and her lips part. I can tell she wants to ask me whether this goes both ways. She'll want to know if I'm fucking anyone else, and if I'm allowed to call in other women whenever *I* need.

"And you will be the only one I see for my needs as well," I tell her to ease any worries and then kiss her. I keep my eyes open and watch as she closes hers. Good girl.

I don't want any other woman. I don't want my hands on

anyone else. I don't want to be inside anyone else. "And if you need anything else. A dress, a dinner out...anything. You'll let me know."

Maddie closes her lips, a smile curving the corners of them. I trace her bottom lip with the pad of my thumb. It sends another throb to my cock, though I've just fucked her.

That's how much I want her.

"We have a deal," she says.

"I like it when you call me Sir," I tell her.

Her lips form a tempting smile as she looks up at me with a devilish and playful spark in her eyes. "We have a deal, Sir."

CHAPTER 8

MADDIE

Smiling, a cup of coffee in one hand and the breeze from the bustling city blowing my hair back, I wait at the cross walk and think back on this past week. Showing up at Graham's office was even better than the 'good idea' Suzette suggested, and so was the safe word.

When I walked in, he looked like he'd been starving. Butterflies bat away in my chest at the memory, and my smile widens. There's no denying it, he's into me. And I'm into him. It's hot and I don't care what anyone else would think...not that I'm shouting it from the rooftops or down the streets of New York City.

It still feels a little scandalous. A little forbidden. I never thought I'd trade my body for rent money. I also never thought

I'd like it so much—this power-play thing that's happening. I freaking love it.

I never thought I'd get addicted to the feeling.

I clear my throat and bury the thoughts away as a work text comes through. I have to pause on the street to answer it.

Even with what's going on between Graham and me, I've been bringing my best to my job as Michael Davies' new assistant.

Suzette made it sound like he just needed one secretary, but it turns out the company is large enough that the CEO has one lead secretary and three assistants. I'm one of the three, and I'm going to stand out if it's the last thing I do. With the text sent, I take a sip of much needed caffeine and continue on, my heels clicking and my confidence rising higher and higher.

It's easier not to think of Graham when I'm actively taking notes, making copies, and answering emails, but every time my mind wanders...

There he is.

I'd be lying if I said I didn't struggle with it at first. The arrangement we made where he took care of my rent had been illicit, something people only do in secret, and I knew I shouldn't go running back once I could handle the rent on my own.

But I wanted him.

I wanted more of him. More of that naughty, illicit

feeling. I wanted to do something dirty. I won't lie, the idea of crawling to him makes me hotter than I thought it ever would. Yet, there's another side that has me questioning if this is wise. It was *more*, and sweeter, and when he'd admitted he wanted me to be there for him—*just* for him and nobody else—my heart almost flew out of my chest. I wonder if he knows how needy he looked at that moment.

I'm not going to tell him. Graham is handsome and charming and rich, and he doesn't want people to know he needs anything. But there's a piece of him that's missing something, and I know I can be that. And I am enjoying every second of it...I'm just a little nervous that I'm the one who's going to fall head over heels and I'm the one who's going to get my heart broken again.

At that thought, I catch him outside walking like he's coming back from a coffee shop, a to-go cup in his hand.

"Isn't it late for coffee?" I call from the crosswalk, a smirk on my face as I toss my own cup into the metal trash can.

Graham looks over at me, not seeming very surprised that we're running into each other. After all, the past few days we have and I'm starting to think it's because he knows my schedule and he's waiting for me. His handsome eyes rake down my dress and my body heats. As they lift to mine, he smirks and responds, "Needed a pick-me-up."

"You're going to be up all night," I tease, twining my fingers together to keep from playing with his tie. It's a dark navy silk number and it suits him well in his crisp gray suit.

He raises his eyebrows. "What's wrong with staying up all night?" His voice is low, throaty, and I love it.

"A man with as much work to do as you have needs his beauty sleep."

"Hmm." He looks down at me just as the wind takes a lock of hair out of the clip I've had it in. He catches it with his finger and tucks it back behind my ear. His touch is like fire and I lean into it. "What are your plans for the evening? Maybe you could help me take the edge off."

"I don't have any," I tell him, my heart fluttering. "Did you have more work to do?"

"I do. A few things need tending to, but I take my work upstairs for the evening," he says. "Care to come up?" The tension between us grows with every passing second we walk to the building. As we step into the elevator I have high hopes...unfortunately it's occupied by an elderly woman so I keep my distance and so does Graham, although our eyes catch in the reflection. With every second, my heart beats a little harder and a little faster, but he doesn't put his hands on me, not even as the woman steps out with a little hum and nod, and the two of us make our way to the penthouse.

It's not lost on me that the first time I ever saw him was in this elevator. I catch him looking at our reflection as it whisks us up, and I bet he's thinking the same thing.

Even as he steps out of the elevator with me following, he

still hasn't touched me. My steps halt before I make it even three steps in.

The view from his living room windows takes my breath away.

"This is stunning," I breathe, unable to help myself as I look out over the city.

Graham comes up behind me and puts his hand on my lower back. My eyes close from the simple contact. I crave his touch like I didn't know I could. "It's the same view you have, my little temptress."

That nickname, with the warmth of his hand on my back, sends pleasant shivers all over my body and I'm all too aware my nipples harden. "It's different up here," I tell him, meeting his gorgeous eyes. A spark ignites and I sink my teeth down into my lower lip.

"Have you ever considered that it's different because you're here?"

"No." I huff the smallest of laughs. "I'm sure it doesn't matter where I am."

"Yes, it does." Graham looks down at me with intensity in his blue eyes. "It matters more than you think."

I'm ready to crawl into his bed and never come out again, but I shake myself out of it. "Did you say you had work to do?"

Regret crosses his face, but he steels himself. "A few things before I'm done for the night."

Graham's penthouse is massive compared to mine. No

surprise, since his takes up the entire top floor and mine is only a small section floors below. A large living room in the middle *reminds* me of mine, only it's wider, with more understated furniture and built-in shelves underneath the floor to ceiling windows. A small office is off to one side, and a hall leading into another section of the penthouse. I can see through to his kitchen and peek into a dining room from here. He waves his hand toward the right. "My bedroom is down that way."

I resist asking him to take me there right now. If I had an hour alone in here, I'd have to explore, because there's so much space and soft, tempting lighting, and I bet he has a private gym and a library, too.

Graham sits at a large, rounded sofa in his living room, his laptop on his lap. At first, I try to sit primly next to him, my feet on the floor and my dress, a simple cream pleated number smoothed over my legs. I kick my heels off and ready myself to tuck my legs under me.

But...

"Is it all right if I put my feet on the sofa?" I ask. I imagine it's far more expensive than anything I've ever owned, and his entire place looks spotless. "This couch is too comfortable."

"That's why I bought it," he says, a smile quirking his mouth. "Put your feet wherever you want."

I tuck my feet up under me and find a blanket spread over the back of the couch. It's lightweight and luxuriously soft, and it feels good to cover my legs.

"What has you working late?"

"Building my empire," he says simply, then taps away at his keyboard for another few minutes. "But I want you here while I work," he murmurs and then looks at me, "so I can have you after as a little reward."

A blush heats my cheeks and I have to look away a moment. When I finally come to my senses I ask him, "A real-estate empire?"

"That's the type." Graham seems to hesitate, his typing getting slower. "I'm working on acquiring a property from a man who doesn't want to sell it to me."

"Why doesn't he want to sell it to you?"

He laughs, the sound a quiet huff. "I don't think he wants to sell it at all, but I can't back down now."

"Why not?"

"Because I've already spent weeks going back and forth in emails and lunch meetings and phone calls. I'm not willing to let it go now that I've made an investment."

My face gets hot. I wonder if he thinks about me the same way—if I'm an investment that he's made, and now wants to get his money's worth. It's as forbidden a thought as fucking him for rent money.

And...hot.

In a way. I shift on the sofa and he notices.

"You're not an investment," Graham says.

I startle next to him. "I didn't…I would never say that… what?"

"Your cheeks got all pink." He lifts a hand from his keyboard and brushes a knuckle over my cheekbone. "I took a guess that you were thinking of yourself as an investment."

"Fine," I admit. "I was…a little bit."

"And what did you think about that?" he questions, his focus entirely on me.

I think…I'd like to be one of his investments. Sought after and taking his attention and focus. Even if it is just to be a reward at the end of a long workday. I think I'd love it.

"I think the idea of being acquired by you is sexy." It takes everything in me to admit, but once it's out, it's more freeing than I thought the admission could be.

"Sexier than paying the rent?" Graham's hand finds its way lower, under the blanket, and to the soft part of my inner thigh. I spread my legs just a little more for him.

"Oh, I don't know." I can barely say the word. My breath is coming too fast. "We could try both."

"What's your safe word, my naive temptress?"

"Red," I say in a heated breath.

"Good girl," he says before kissing me, and in a single moment I'm swept away in his touch. My head is fuzzy with lust. His hands are everywhere at once, his lips never stopping. He consumes every inch of my neck and lips. I'm barely cognizant as he strips me down to nothing and he fucks me over the edge of the sofa, facing the big picture windows, sliding inside me with hard, fast strokes. Graham makes me come that way, too, with his hand wrapping around and stroking over my belly until his fingertips find their way lower to circle my clit. He has to hold me in this position because my knees are weak and shaky. With every hard stroke I climb higher and higher until pleasure wraps itself around both of us at the same time. I'm breathless and stunned, really, by the time he's planting small kisses on my neck and settling everything back into place. When it's over he pulls me back into his lap and folds his arms around me. He plants a kiss and then another. It's silent as he leaves me on the couch, zips up his pants, and hands me what I need to get dressed again.

He sits next to me as he was before, although his arm is around me this time. I'm cuddled up to his side and he reaches for his laptop, reminding me that he has work to do.

"I thought...do you want me to stay?" I gather up the courage to ask him as the moment seems to come to a close.

"Yes." His answer is simple, and I start to feel out of place. "If you're available and don't mind that I'll be working," he adds.

I settle myself into his side, enjoying the warmth and comfort and simply nod.

The evening is easy. I have a few messages I answer on my phone and for the most part, I'm able to lay into him in comfortable silence, his laptop ticking away as he occasionally asks me questions. Sometimes he asks if I need anything, like the champagne he brings me. Sometimes he asks questions like whether I prefer tea or coffee and what restaurants I like in the city.

As the night gets later, his touches become more focused on my curves and he lingers longer. Two glasses of champagne down and his laptop closes. He pushes it back on the coffee table and then murmurs something about 'earning this' before his lips press to mine and his body covers mine. When we fuck this time, he's on top of me with my legs spread around his hips. The climax is higher and heavier than the last, and he groans my name into my neck just as I cry out his with the blinding pleasure.

I'm breathless and the most at ease I've ever been as I lie down on the sofa with my back to his front and the blanket wrapped around us. An old movie is playing on the TV; the New York skyline surrounds us.

"What do you think?" I ask after a while. "Worth the investment?" A small smile tugs at my lips.

"Every single penny," he says, and kisses the back of my neck. The simple kiss feels like heaven.

Time passes easily. The two of us finding out little pieces of each other, and each night falling into a steady rhythm.

We don't only have sex, which is what I imagined originally, though I'm sure that given a week without any obligations, we probably could. I can't get enough of him and the same seems to be true of him.

Graham takes me to get coffee in the mornings. And if he isn't there, I find a text on my phone telling me to have a good day and that there's a coffee waiting at the front desk for me.

Although the mornings have been the same, tonight is a little different.

He texts me before I leave the office and asks me if I want to meet for dinner. I expect someplace too fancy for my work clothes, but he takes me to an Italian place I told him once that I loved. "You really haven't been here?" I tease over our entrées.

It's not high-end, but it's authentic and the atmosphere is amazing. He simply shakes his head, folding the cloth napkin in his lap. With the candles lit on the table and the soft din of conversation around us, I can't help but think how romantic it feels.

"I usually come with my family. My aunt loves pasta and we're very close," I tell him casually and have a sip of the cabernet he ordered. "You should bring your parents." It's divine, so delicious that I almost miss his reaction.

Graham glances at me, his eyes guarded. "I see…" He trails off and doesn't say anything for a few minutes. For the first time, insecurity sweeps through me. It's sudden, but enough that I feel it in the tips of my fingers. I set the glass down and swallow thickly.

"I'm sorry if I said something out of line."

"You didn't." He twirls his fork over his plate, seeming to decide what to say. "I was close to my parents as well."

There's a *but* at the end of that sentence that Graham doesn't say.

"My dad died young, and my mother couldn't live without him. They're both gone."

"Oh, Graham." I reach for his hand across the table and squeeze it. "I'm so sorry. I didn't know."

He opens his mouth like he might reassure me and say it was a long time ago, but instead he says a quiet *thank you.*

We sit for a minute. Silverware clinks against plates at the tables around us. Faint noises from the kitchen float out to our table. I wish I could think of something to say but all I can think of is, "I'm happy to be here with you."

He offers me a smile but doesn't say anything else. I take another sip of wine, attempting to start any conversation.

"I feel awful," I admit to him and he tells me not to.

"According to a good friend of mine, it's why I work as much as I do. I wanted to make sure that never happened to me," Graham continues. "I wanted to make sure I had my life under control. Nobody would be able to run me into the ground."

He clears his throat and then says, "He says I work too much. I tell him he's just mad I make more than him." He attempts to joke, and I smile back at him, letting this admission sink in.

I run my thumb over his knuckles, considering my next words. This arrangement doesn't mean that we have the kind of relationship where I can comment on his choices. But I've seen how he works. I know he pushes himself beyond the regular working hours.

"Do you ever go on vacation?"

He laughs, his blue eyes crinkling. "I live in a penthouse in one of the most beautiful buildings in Manhattan. I'm always on vacation compared to the life my parents had."

I laugh along with him, but…I understand the sentiment. I get what it's like to struggle and not have enough money and always worry about making ends meet.

I also know that fixing it is hard work, and it's the kind of work you can't keep doing forever. Everybody needs a break sometimes, even if your father's life was objectively harder.

"Would you ever consider going on a vacation? A real one, I mean."

I keep my voice casual and take a sip of wine, watching Graham's face like this is just a getting-to-know-you conversation.

He watches me back, his eyes hot.

"Up until a few weeks ago, I probably wouldn't have. I don't see the point of being out of the office when I'm just going to take my work to another location."

The pause between us suddenly feels charged and even hotter than it did before. I can feel the flush coming to my face. Hopefully, Graham doesn't notice how often I blush around him. It's not because we're falling in love or anything, it's just because he's incredibly attractive and everything that comes out of his mouth turns me on.

Which might mean we're falling in love.

Or at least I'm falling in...*something* with him. Want, maybe. I'm falling into a much deeper want than the beginning, when all I could think about was not getting kicked out of my apartment.

"What about now?"

"Now..." He wets his bottom lip with the tip of his tongue. "Now, I might consider it, if the right offer came along."

"The right offer?" I question as my brows knit. My pulse feels like it's going too fast to actually pump blood, and I'm getting lightheaded. If I wanted to know for sure how Graham felt about me, I'd say...*if I asked?*

But I'm not sure I'm ready to know.

"If the right man asked me if I wanted to go somewhere with him, I'd think about going on a vacation...somewhere," I offer instead.

Something flickers across his face. "What kinds of places do you like to vacation to? Would you rather ski or lie on the beach?"

I answer with a smile and with the tips of my fingers slipping around the stem of the glass. "Anywhere I can wear a bikini."

"I like the sound of that. You can't wear one when you're skiing, though, so I guess Vail is out."

"That's where you're wrong. They have a *lot* of hot tubs there. I could spend practically the whole time in a bikini or at the spa while you...play in the snow?" I guess and he laughs, a deep husky laugh that soothes whatever part of me was concerned.

"I enjoy skiing and I do believe there is a spa I could leave you while I 'play in the snow.'"

The night carried on easily and when it was time to take me home, he did so like a gentleman, leaving me with a kiss and something else that made me feel like we took a small step forward in a direction I didn't know we would go.

The next week, Graham texts me when I'm in for the evening and I can't help but to smile.

Graham: Looking at some vacation spots. Can I get your opinion?

Maddie: Of course.

Graham: Come upstairs

Diligently, I take the elevator upstairs to the penthouse. Graham gave me a keycard that lets me onto the top floor, and when I get there, he's on his comfortable couch where he's already fucked me half a dozen times, his computer on the coffee table, and he's looking up places to vacation.

I cuddle in next to him, as I'm getting far too comfortable doing, and he angles his laptop toward me.

"The Virgin Islands," he says, and scrolls past gorgeous photos of cabanas next to a sparkling blue ocean. "Or there are some places closer that could be fun, and we could spend a week or two enjoying each other."

My heart does a little twist in my chest, that insecurity very much riding through me again. "A weekend getaway is probably all I could manage right now with my job."

He glances at me, reading my expression and then nods as if it's an easy answer.

"A weekend it is then." Graham scrolls through a few more resort listings. "In this hypothetical vacation, I think we should lie in the sun and enjoy drinks and the sound of the ocean."

We echoes in my head and makes me hot all over.

"Oh yeah? Is that what we should do?"

"For now…" He closes the laptop, sets it aside, and kisses me. "I think we should relax."

"Did you realize you were tired?" I ask him and he leaves me a moment, only laughing at my question as he goes to the kitchen. I watch as he opens a bottle of champagne and pours us each a glass.

It's only after he's back next to me, each of us sipping the bubbly, that he admits, "I do think I could use a moment to sleep in, and"—he lowers his voice, planting a small kiss on the crook of my neck before whispering in the shell of my ear—"enjoy my investments."

As I inhale his masculine scent, his eyes reach mine and the kiss we share in that moment is perfect. Everything is perfect with him. It's almost too good to be true and I find myself hushing that voice in the back of my head.

I anticipate him taking me again, but instead we lie down and relax into each other.

We relax so much that he ends up sprawled on the couch, his arms around me. I let my head rest on his chest and listen to his heartbeat for so long that Graham falls asleep.

He looks younger when he's sleeping, and it tugs at my heart.

I want to pull the throw blanket over both of us and stay all night, but thoughts race in my mind.

The way he talked about his parents and getting more from his life makes me hesitate. There's a decent chance he doesn't want anything serious because of this, and I don't want to be the one to get in his way.

And...I don't want to be the one who falls in love too fast.

That little voice in my head says it's already too late.

I slip out of his arms anyway, tuck the blanket around him, and go back down to the eighth floor. Back down to reality where I can't sleep because I'm almost certain I'm way in over my head, over my heels, and all the way back around again.

CHAPTER 9

MADDIE

At the end of the month, nearly five weeks of seeing each other, if you can call it that, Graham whisks me away on vacation. I know from experience that there are plenty of beautiful sunny places to visit on the coast, but it hardly feels like five minutes on the private plane before we're touching down.

I spent most of the ride with his mouth on mine or sipping champagne and enjoying the little touches so that helped pass the time.

The beach house he rented for the weekend is so close to the water that I hear every wave that rolls in. It's minimalist, with everything nearly white so the view holds even more impact. Palm trees bend in the breeze. The air smells like ocean salt, and Graham strips off his dress shirt almost immediately and takes me into a massive bedroom overlooking the sea.

There are three lingerie sets on the bed already: one pink, one red, one black.

"Your choice, temptress."

A blush rises through me and I can't help but think this is a fantasy I never dared dream before. One a girl like me couldn't have even imagined.

Graham stands with his hands on my waist while I look them over, pulling me into him. I can already feel how hard he is and how hard he has been since we were on the plane. My whole body is hot with how much he obviously wants me.

"Black."

He lifts the lacy lingerie off the bed and puts it into my hands. "Go change," he says. "Then come back to me."

My heart races as I ready myself and slip on the lingerie. It's beautiful and expensive, and when I'm wearing it, I really do look like a temptress.

I feel like one, too.

The sun is on an angle in the sky when I pad back out into the bathroom, completely enamored by everything about the present moment. Graham sits on the edge of the bed, in a suit that makes him look all the more powerful, his knees spread and his hands clasped between them. His eyes darken at the sight of me in the things he bought.

"Fuck," he says softly, his gaze wandering down my body

as if he's undressing me with the simple action. "Strip for me."

I work my fingers under the straps and peel the lace away from my skin. I just put it on a few minutes ago, but it already feels like it's part of me. Graham bites his lip when the lace comes away from my nipple. They tighten in the cool of the air conditioning, and he motions for me to turn around while I work the panties over my hips and down to the floor.

"Bend," he says.

The cool air touches a soft, wet part of me, and Graham groans.

"Come here, temptress. Bring the lingerie."

It feels strangely small in my hands as I cross the room and step between his knees. All the while I can barely control my breathing. All I want is him to take me. Graham's hands find my hair, and he pulls my face to his and kisses me. It starts out hot and gets hotter, his tongue exploring my mouth and my body going into overdrive. It always makes me want more, but Graham only deepens the kiss, teasing me, taking his time while his hands roam over my waist and my nipples and the curves of my ass.

I'm out of breath when he finally takes the lingerie out of my hands and wraps the larger piece around my eyes.

With the lace folded over so many times, I can't see anything. It only adds to the tension that rolls through my body. *I need him.* I almost tell him but instead I swallow the confession.

His knuckles brushing over my ribs come as a welcome surprise, goosebumps spread all down the front of my body. His lips press against my collarbone. He works his way up the side of my neck, and then he shifts, pushing me onto the bed. He puts me on my hands and knees, my ass in the air, and gently slips a pillow under my stomach to prop me up.

"What—"

I don't get a chance to ask the rest of my question before his hands are on my hips and his mouth is between my legs. I've never been eaten out from this position and it's intoxicating and new and mind-blowing. My inner thighs shake. Heat concentrates between my legs, where his tongue is running over every inch of me and licking inside me. His hands stay firm on my hips until he uses them to spread me open a little farther. Every nerve ending across every inch of my skin is on high alert as the pleasure builds and builds.

I'm collapsed onto the bed, my head in my arms, and don't realize at first that his tongue is moving *up*.

It brushes against my hole and I tense, but Graham doesn't let me move. "Stay how you are, temptress. I want all of you."

"Okay."

"Good girl."

My mind is already overwhelmed by his mouth, and the feeling only intensifies as he licks my hole. I'm a mess, trying to push my hips back into his face, and it takes me a few seconds to realize he's pulled away.

A bottle clicks.

Something cool lands between my spread cheeks, and then Graham's circling my hole with his fingertips.

"Good girl," he murmurs in a deep tone coated with lust, though I haven't done anything but remained still. I'm trembling over a pillow, caught between wanting to come and wanting to stay in this hot, liquid feeling forever. "I'm going to put my fingers inside you. Get you ready. Have you ever taken like this before?"

"No," I gasp with my heart pounding.

He makes a pleased sound. "Don't worry, temptress. I'll help you. What's your safe word?"

"Red," I answer him, and he tells me what a good girl I am for him and how good it's going to feel. My nails dig into the comforter with anticipation.

He slides one finger into me slow, coaxing me to keep breathing. It burns a little, and when I make a noise, he adds more lube and keeps fucking me with that finger. His other hand slides between my legs. It feels so *full* and so *hot* and the pleasure builds inside of me like I've never felt before.

The second his fingers meet my clit, my inhibitions fall away. I can't concentrate on two things at once and my head thrashes. Graham circles my clit slowly, patiently, reminding me to stay where he put me, and it's all I can do not to try and fuck his hand. I get used to the finger in my asshole and moan, wanting more, wanting to come.

He adds another finger.

I don't mean to ride them, but it happens anyway. I want sensation any way I can get it. His fingers on my clit and inside me. It feels shockingly sinful, when he's rubbing like that, keeping my desire at a steady level.

The third finger is still hard to take.

"Please," I beg. "Let me come."

"When I'm all the way inside you," he says, voice soothing. "You can do that for me, can't you?"

"Yes." I rock my hips back toward him. "Graham. Fuck me. I can't wait any longer."

"You can," he murmurs.

He makes me wait.

He keeps fucking me with three fingers. They're thick, stretching me, and I bury my face in my arms and pant. I didn't realize it would be so much, but I never want to stop.

"What's your safe word, temptress?"

It takes a lot of effort to think of words at a time like this. "Red."

"Remember," he warns. "I'm going to fuck your ass. Stay relaxed for me."

He pulls his fingers out of my ass, and my heart climbs up into my throat. It's quiet for a moment and then the bed groans as he positions himself. I've never done this before. I'm not totally convinced that I *can*. But then his hands stroke down my hips, spreading me, and the head of his cock nudges against my lubed hole.

"Push back," he says softly.

I do it, my breath stuttering at how impossibly big he feels.

Graham fucks into me slowly, with as much patience as he used to kiss me, and when he finally slides inside I gasp at the stretch and my entire body lights on fire.

"I'll let you adjust," he says as my heart pounds. I struggle to take him and his hand trails back down between my legs, finding my clit.

The pleasure and the stretch are both so intense that I grab for anything I can reach. The only thing to hold is the blankets, so I curl my fingers around them and hold on, trying to breathe. I don't know what I want to do. Rock back against him, I think, but I don't know if I can take anymore.

His fingers on my clit make the decision for me.

I want to move with them so much that I tilt my hips forward, and when I move them back, another inch of Graham enters me.

"You're beautiful like this," he says, his voice strained, and I don't know if I believe him but I can't do a thing about it. All I can do is breathe into the covers. His fingers speed up on my clit and I rock back harder, taking more of him.

I get lost in the movement, surrendering to the stretch and the effort, and Graham grunts. "There," he says. "That's all of me, good girl."

I grind back on him, begging for more contact with his

fingers. They work me faster as he pulls out and thrusts back in.

Over and over, steadily increasing in pace.

Everything goes hazy with pleasure beyond control.

My orgasm builds and builds until it explodes and every single inch of me clenches down on Graham.

"That's it temptress," he murmurs at the shell of my ear as I shake out my orgasm. He feels even bigger inside me, too big, and I brace myself on the bed as he pushes in as deep as he can and comes with the sexiest groan I've ever heard in my life.

It's hot inside me, and he feels so big I almost can't stand it, and every part of me shakes and shakes and shakes.

A short time later, Graham pulls out. I let him go with a hiss. He unties the blindfold with gentle hands, takes me in his arms, and then we're moving. Toward the bathroom, hopefully. Toward a really long bath. I need it for my wrung-out muscles.

He kisses my forehead. "You were so good."

So were you, I think about saying, but can't make it happen.

I barely remember dinner when I wake up the next morning. Graham strokes my hair and gives me new outfits to choose from and checks emails while I take a shower almost as long as the bath then dry my hair until it shines and put on the brand-new sundress he gave me.

Then we go out into the sunny resort town and stroll the

sidewalks.

It's a dream vacation, really. The main street is quaint and busy with people coming in and out of shops, a lot of them obviously enjoying some time away from home.

My only problem is the soreness.

I hold Graham's hand as we walk past stores and restaurants, my thighs aching and my ass even more.

"That's nice," he says, nodding his head toward some art in a gallery window. "What do you think?"

"I think I need to slow down," I whisper.

He takes my chin in his hand and tilts my face toward his, his gaze intense and concerned. "What's wrong?"

"I'm sore," I admit with a laugh. "From last night."

Graham takes us to the edge of the sidewalk so we won't be in anyone's way and puts his hands on my waist. "You know that you can use your safe word without consequence, don't you?"

"Of course I do."

"How sore are you?"

I've been trying to ignore the pain, but...it's more than I thought it would be. "A lot," I tell him. "It was my first time, so maybe..."

"There are things we can do about that." He steers me to the nearest cafe and orders me an iced tea, sitting me firmly on one of the padded outdoor seats. "I'll be right back," Graham says. "Don't move."

When he comes back five minutes later, there's a packet of ibuprofen in his hand. He opens it with his teeth and watches while I swallow down two of the pills.

"We'll sit here until it starts to kick in," he says, then takes the seat next to me and holds my hand.

"I'm really okay," I promise, but he shakes his head, still worried about me.

That makes me feel as warm and loved as I did last night.

Loved. I shouldn't be thinking that word. I swallow it down and focus on feeling better.

I finish my iced tea, and when we step back onto the sidewalk, I can't help tipping my face up to kiss him. I feel a thousand times better with the painkiller, and it's wonderful to be out in the sun without anything to think about but relaxing together.

The kiss turns hot, Graham's hand coming up to grip my chin, and someone nearby shouts. "Cute couple!"

Graham picks his head up, his eyes narrow, a smile curving his lips only slightly. "Thank you." All the while my heart races and my body heats. *Couple.*

I watch him with emotions storming through my chest. I shouldn't want him to agree this badly. Maybe I just wanted to hear what it sounds like for him to say *yes, she's mine* in public.

Graham looks back down at me, his expression softening. "Ready to shop?" he asks.

"I'm ready," I tell him.

I don't tell him I'm ready for much more.

CHAPTER 10

GRAHAM

Brian: *Come on, we want to meet her.*

I stare at the text. Brian's message sits in my phone unanswered.

Brian: *Just do it.*

The sigh that leaves me as I stare out the window from my penthouse is filled with both agitation and apprehension. I shouldn't have fucking told Brian anything. He badgered me for an update and now this. I watch the cars move below me before deciding to text her.

It seems to me that it could be woven into the verbal contract that she would accompany me to social gatherings. After all, I do enjoy her company. The small sighs she makes when something romantic happens on the television and the way she bites down on her bottom lip, her brow scrunched, when she gets an email from work that something didn't go well. It's...noticeable and quite distracting in a good way. I find myself enjoying her and it's quite possible she'll fill a need within my friend group as well.

Graham: *You have plans tonight?*

Maddie: *Tonight?*

Graham: *I need a date.*

Maddie: *Ooh, a date for what?*

I can practically hear her response. The touch of excitement. It warms something inside of me and I bite the bullet. Why shouldn't I after all? She's mine when I desire and if it's something she doesn't prefer, we'll make that accommodation.

Graham: *I'm getting together with my friends. Three of us. Small group, but they're bringing their wives.*

Three dots bounce on the screen while she types his answer.

Maddie: *You can't be the only one there by yourself.*

Graham: *That's what I thought.*

Graham: *Will you join me?*

Maddie: *Of course I will. What time?*

Graham: *I'll stop by your place at seven.*

Maddie: *See you then.*

The moment she agrees, there's a relief that's unreliable, but it's quickly followed by unwanted nerves. I shake them off and do the best I can to focus, but for the rest of the day all I'm able to think about is whether or not she'll enjoy herself tonight and what Brian and the others will think of her. It's unsettling and given that I've never brought a date or had a girlfriend I've been interested in long enough to introduce to my friends, I'm not quite sure how to get rid of the anxiousness or what to do with it. I remind myself she's not my girlfriend, this is different. Even if it all goes to hell, I can simply keep them separate.

It's not until I knock on her door, wearing a suit and tie with no jacket, and she opens it that all apprehension falls away.

Her little black dress and kitten heels are both casual and yet elegant.

"Is this all right?" she questions, and I murmur that she's perfect. She's stunning. Once again I find myself wrapped up in Madelyn Cunnigham. It's odd how everything slips into place when she's with me. How the uncertainty fades away. She puts her arm through mine, and I guide her to the elevator and then into my private car. I find myself thinking I would feel even more at ease and these little hiccups like earlier wouldn't occur if she would move in with me.

I recall her stipulation about time apart initially but that was weeks ago, and I'm almost certain she'd agree things have been easy between us and that we are spending more and more time together. With the streets dark and the city lights surrounding us, I take glances at Madelyn the entire drive to the restaurant, wondering what she would say if I offered.

MADDIE

All the nervousness in my belly keeps me relatively quiet, although I have a million questions on my mind.

Graham lays his hand palm up in the middle of the seats and I slip my hand into place. I can't help but smile as he rubs soothing circles on my wrists as if he can sense I'm nervous.

"So. Tell me about your friends. Have you known them a long time?" My heart pounds as he nods.

I almost ask him, 'this isn't like a test or anything right?' but then my lips slam shut. *A test of what?* We enjoy what we're doing and that's all there is to it, I lie to myself, knowing damn well this is different but not wanting to jinx it.

Graham answers more thoroughly, "I've known Scott and Drew since college and Brian since grade school. We've never lost touch. I don't have siblings, so they're the closest thing I have to brothers."

My throat gets tight at the subtle emotion in his voice. "That's really nice, Graham. My friend Suzette is like that. Basically a sister to me."

"Suzette?"

"Maybe you could meet her sometime," I offer. "I owe her a drink since she helped me get my new job."

He hesitates, then says, "I'd like that."

"I would, too." I scramble around for another question before the conversation can get too deep. "Do you get together with these friends often?" The car hums as we move through traffic.

"A few times a year." Graham says and then confides in me a little more and the small talk is more than helpful.

My nerves settle as he tells me more about his friends, the classes they took in college, and the things they got up to on the weekends. The driver pulls us into a curved drive that takes us off the city street and close to the door as we arrive at the restaurant.

It's on the first floor of a skyscraper with manicured plants in the front and lights glowing above the windows. A pristine awning covers a door made from dark wood that shines like it's been polished. Uniformed valets wait to park cars for people, and everything I can see looks freshly painted and lovingly maintained.

"Wow," I breathe. "This is a *nice* place." I nervously look down at my dress and wonder if I should have opted for something more...delicate or detailed or higher heels. I've been to a number of high-end banquets for charities and exquisite dinners and events with my ex, but this is...*more*.

"You look beautiful," Graham says, and offers me his arm. "Stunning even," he adds with a charming smirk that eases my mind.

He holds my hand in his as the hostess takes us through the restaurant. We walk past people at candlelit tables to a private room in the back. Graham's friends sit at a long table with their wives. When we step inside, all of them get up from the table to shake Graham's hand, slap his back, and sneak in hugs. The atmosphere is easy and friendly. They're more than welcoming.

"Graham, who's this?" one of his friends asks, barely concealed excitement in his eyes. "You've never brought a date before."

A blush heats my cheeks and I do everything I can to not let my nerves show as I give a little wave.

Graham rolls his eyes. "I told you I was bringing someone. Everyone, this is Maddie. Maddie, this is everybody." He goes around, telling me his friends' names and the names of their partners. The man who asked the question is Scott. He's tall and has dark hair like Graham. Drew has lighter hair and a quick smile. Brian's a redhead with a big laugh.

I know I'm supposed to play a part—to fill the space so Graham doesn't have to be the only single one here—but as soon as we sit down at the table, it all starts to feel...*real*.

All Graham's friends are married, and all the wives are friendly, open, and funny, and they include me in their group without hesitation. It's easy to imagine how it would be if I was Graham's wife and not just his stand-in date.

Too easy.

I remind myself throughout the night that this is fake. They call me his girlfriend and I swallow down the lie as I answer their questions.

Graham brushes his knuckles over the back of my neck as everyone's chatting between dinner and dessert. It's an affectionate gesture. It's casual and intimate, and I *like* it.

"You okay?" he asks in a low voice as the appetizers are passed around the table and dinner menus are swept away. "Having a good time?"

"The best time," I answer honestly, trying not to think too much. Doing my best to simply play my part and not let my heart make my head think this is something it isn't.

"Really? Because we could duck out early, if you're not."

"Your friends are great." On an impulse, I lean in and kiss his cheek. It's a risk I can't help but take. As he smiles down at me, a friend at the end of the table tells him to get a room and I blush violently. The table laughs and I laugh along too, and as the night goes on, with every small kiss and touch from Graham, I feel less and less like a fraud.

CHAPTER 11

MADDIE

Nearly two months of this arrangement have passed and everything seems just perfect. It's like a dream I didn't dare to dream before. Without the cost of rent, my job is more than enough to keep me afloat and contribute back to my savings. I don't have a worry in the world, other than how so much of this new world of mine is reliant on Graham. Just like it used to be with my ex.

I swallow down that thought as often as it comes up and focus on the positives.

Meeting Graham's friends has definitely either taken us to the next level or given me mixed signals. That combined with little trips on private jets for weekend vacations in the sun...life is very much too good to be true.

I've been added to a group chat with Julie, Bee, and Whitney, and they're just as lovely, welcoming, and funny as they were at the dinner. They're very interested in Graham and me, but I keep it light and vague. Although for the most part, I don't have to hide anything. Like when they ask how long we've been together or how we met. Eight weeks and in an elevator in his building. Oh how they thought that was scandalous...if only they really knew.

Between time with Suzette after work, an after-hours meeting to schedule a charity function, and Graham leaving town twice for meetings, before I know it, the week has gone by and I haven't seen him.

He's busy and I'm busy, and even though the ache I feel when I think about being with him doesn't go away, I get lost in my life for the first time in a long time. Lost in a good way, this time. Not the way I was lost with Kevin, when the days started to blur together and the only thing that broke it up was getting engaged. Which obviously ended worse than it began.

It feels like a century ago that I was worried about the rent and made that frantic call to Graham. It almost feels like a new life, even though I'm living in the same apartment.

I want it to stay like this, all new and exciting, for as long as possible.

I want things to stay okay. I think, this time, it might stick.

Since I haven't heard from Kenzie, my needy cousin, in about a week and a half, my aunt tells me she's doing much better. Some small part of me thinks that it might not be a good thing that my cousin hasn't messaged, but I can't bring myself to worry about it when I'm finally in a decent place.

Worrying never helps anyone, anyway. One of the best parts of all this is that my optimism doesn't feel so hard, now that I have a job and Graham and a group chat with another group of women who I can really see myself being friends with.

Friday after work, I come home from the office at the end of the day and find a paper taped to the door of my apartment.

My heart jumps into my throat and my blood goes cold. In my experience, sheets of paper taped to your apartment door never mean anything good, but as soon as I swallow down my knee-jerk reaction, I realize it's too small to be an official notice. The paper is too nice, too.

Actually, it's a note from Graham on a page torn from the pad on his desk. It's thick, heavy paper with his monogram on the top.

I want to see you. Come up when you get this. I've missed you.

That's all it says.

I peel the paper off the door, dislodging the tape he used to keep it there, and run my fingertips over the words. This feels different. He could've just texted me, or called, and told me he wanted to see me. Leaving a note in his handwriting, though...

It means he wrote the note and came up here, thinking of me. It means he pressed the tape to the top of the paper and looked it over before he left. He stood here in the hall, wondering when I'd be home to see it.

It means he knew that anyone could walk by and see this.

No, he didn't sign his name, but they'd see that someone with bold, clean handwriting wanted someone else enough to tape a note to their door.

That probably shouldn't make me as giddy as it does. It probably doesn't mean as much as I think it does. But still, I remind myself, I'm allowed to be a hopeless romantic, even in a not-so-romantic arrangement like this, so long as I protect my heart.

I rush inside, tuck the note on my bedside table, and change out of my work clothes. I think Graham likes my work clothes—his eyes go dark every time he sees me coming through the lobby or meets me for drinks after—but it's Friday, and I've been in those outfits all week. I choose a flowy dress instead and a beautiful pair of emerald earrings Graham bought me while we were on vacation and take the elevator up to the penthouse. It's my first time wearing them, they stay in a trinket tray on my bedside safe and sound so I don't lose them. But today feels like a special day and for that, I choose the beautiful earrings that feel just as special.

The elevator lets me directly into the wide, spacious entryway, which looks over his kitchen and the big living room with the stunning view of the city. I've been here several times, and I know it shouldn't be anything special considering

I live in the building, but it is. Everything about this space is just what I would have imagined for a man like Graham. It's clean and beautiful and classy, and the best part of it is him.

Or it would be if I could see him.

I pause, closing the door quietly behind me, and listen. He said he wanted to see me and to come up, so I know he's in here.

After a second, I hear his voice floating in from one of the other rooms. I kick off my heels, leaving them at the entryway, and follow the low rumble past the spacious kitchen with Graham's shiny, expensive espresso machine that I know how to use now; past the sitting room with the *very* comfortable sofa that costs more than furniture should and the TV that rises out of a hidden compartment so it doesn't block the view; and past the original art framed on the wall that Graham got at an auction after he bought his first New York property.

These things mean more than they did the first time I was here. He's told me enough to know that he doesn't choose things without a reason, another fact about him that gives me butterflies.

He thinks about me even more carefully.

Graham doesn't have to say that for me to know it. He's always considerate when we go out, despite the dirty deal he offered me to pay the rent.

Could that have been fake, somehow? Not the deal itself—that definitely wasn't fake given I'm the one who technically offered it. The more Graham and I spend time with each other, the less I think he's the kind of guy who'd ever do it again. He's said in passing it was reckless for us and I agree. And Graham isn't a reckless kind of man.

I swallow down nervousness. I don't know if these feelings will ever go away. I'm not concerned that he'll end things between us when I don't see it coming. I'm more nervous about impressing him and living up to his expectations. I want him to enjoy this in the same way I do.

I *really* want to impress him, because...

I don't want this to end.

It doesn't escape me that when this ends, he'll be the one doing it. And I don't think I'll see it coming. I take a deep breath and promise myself not to think about *any* of this ending. Setting a timeline hasn't been what this is about. That's why we have a safe word, and why he seemed so relieved to see me in his office for the second rent payment. That memory goes a long way to soothe my nerves every time they creep up.

We can do this for as long as we want.

Graham is in a smaller, cozier den at one side of the penthouse. He sits on what I now know is his favorite working chair, an elbow propped on the arm, the phone to his ear. It's a worn brown leather that fits the masculine natural tones of the room.

"Go into more detail about that," he says. "I'm not sure I know enough to give you an answer you'll be satisfied with."

His tone is confident and commanding on the phone. The cadence of his voice sends a shiver down my spine. Nobody I've met before makes me feel like they could take charge of just about anything in the world and make it better than it was before.

Nobody would look as hot as Graham doing it, either. The natural light from the large, paned windows accentuates his perfect features and the way his clothes fit his body like they were made for him.

Which they were.

I pad quietly in through the door and he turns his head. His blue eyes brighten when he sees me, then immediately get darker as his pupils expand.

Then it's just like the first time I saw him in the elevator. My heart goes a little crazy over how attractive he is. Something electric about the air around him makes my chest get hot, and it feels like I've gotten an intense crush on this man in the space of seconds. It's been longer than that, obviously, but stepping into any room he's in makes it all feel new again.

I give him a little wave and mouth *I can go if you're busy.*

He shakes his head and readjusts in his seat, spreading his legs wider all the while staring at me. "That's something I considered, but only in the context of—yes, that's right."

I can almost feel him undressing me. Imagine his hands pulling my dress over my head. Feel his fingertips drag when he does it. This man hasn't even touched me and yet my body can already feel what he'll do to me. That's the power he has over me and I freaking love it.

I take two steps toward him, and Graham holds up a hand. I freeze in place, my face hot. He mouths the command, *strip*.

Every nerve ending in my body lights ablaze. I do as he commands, slowly, like I know he likes. Letting the dress fall to a puddle of cloth on the floor. He stops me before I can unsnap my bra and slip off my panties. They're a matching nude lace duo. Apparently he wants me to keep them on.

He slowly holds up one finger, then points at the floor.

I put my hand over my mouth to cover my gasp.

Crawl, he mouths, still pointing at the floor. He looks down, like he needs to emphasize the point, then looks back up at me, his eyes moving slowly over my nearly naked body.

"Right," he says, his voice shocking me into action. "My plan is to recoup the investment through a series of targeted improvements. I'm not talking about razing the place to the ground. That would be a waste."

I sink slowly to my knees, feeling the pattern of the rug press against my skin, then lower my hands to the floor.

This is so hot, on the verge of degrading or maybe submission, that I have to stop and take a few deep breaths.

Graham snaps his fingers.

It's one small sound and it draws my whole attention to him. His blue eyes are intense on mine as I begin to crawl across the rug.

He never looks away from me, even as he continues his conversation. It sounds to me like he's talking about the deal he's been working on—the one that's been keeping him up at night, the one he can't let go of even when it annoys the hell out of him—and it makes crawling across the floor even sexier. If he wants me to know about this conversation, he'll tell me about it later.

What he wants more is to watch me crawl to him.

I take my time, making each movement as slow and languid as I can. I'm a foot away from him, maybe less, when Graham spreads his knees and unzips his pants.

My mouth waters and my breathing quickens as I settle between his feet.

Graham takes his cock out and runs his fist over it, biting his hip. "That's fine," he says, voice terse. "I'm switching over to my people now. Email me with anything else you need."

He pauses, watching me, his hand still moving on his cock. He's thick and long, and I'm far too eager to give him everything he wants.

"I'm off the call," he says, and then he rattles off a list of details. I don't really hear any of them. I'm too busy watching his hand. On the next downstroke, I lean in and lick his tip. The slit already has a bead of precum, and I lick it away before hollowing my cheeks and taking his head into my mouth. He's smooth and already hard as iron. I cover my teeth with my lips and take more of him in.

Graham chokes back a groan. "Whatever you think. Just get it done."

He hangs up and tosses his phone to the side. It bounces off the chair and falls to the carpet. Then his hands are in my hair and he guides me down his cock.

He's so hard that he must've been thinking about this all day. If I'd known that note was on my door, I'd have thought about it all day, too. Graham's hips thrust up as I take him deeper, my throat fluttering around him.

"Fuck," he says, his voice strained. "Your mouth feels so fucking good."

I continue, and his hands work through my hair and gather it away from my face so it doesn't get in the way. I lick every inch of him that I can reach. I wrap one hand around his base and stroke. It's wet and messy and I know damn well my lips will be swollen, my lipstick ruined. But to hear that groan and the way his breath hitches, *I fucking love it.*

My eyes sting and water as I take more of him down, eager to get him off.

Graham groans again and tells me to be a good girl and take it.

It doesn't take much effort to stop my movements, not when he starts pumping into my mouth, holding my head gently while he does it.

After a minute he stops, pulling my head away. His abs bunch up below the waistband of his pants. His shirt is an untucked mess. Graham closes his eyes and breathes.

When he opens them again, all I can see his how much he wants me.

"Maddie," he says, running the pad of his thumb over my cheekbone.

"Hi," I breathe, not knowing what else to say and not caring.

He growls, and the next thing I know I'm being lifted off the floor and arranged on the chair on my knees, gripping the back of the chair. He rips the lace of my underwear at my entrance as he kisses my neck and tells me he's wanted me all day. The fabric of Graham's pants brushes against the backs of my thighs, and then he's pushing into me, his fingers stroking my clit.

"You're so fucking wet." His first stroke is deep and hard and takes my breath away. "Did you think of me when you were at that office?" He questions between kisses down my neck and then shoulders.

"All day," I tell him because it's true. Every time I finished a task or started a new one or got a drink or ate my lunch or stapled some documents, I thought of him. He rakes his teeth over my shoulder, and I admit in a rushed breath, "I missed you."

"You should have told me," he scolds, and fucks into me harder. With a hand on my hip and the other gripping the back of my neck, he pounds into me.

I dig my fingers into the leather and nearly bite down on the back of it to stifle my moans. His fingers are taking me right to the edge. I can feel my orgasm gathering, centered over my clit and deep inside me. "Would you have come to the office and taken me?" I question, although I'm nearly breathless.

"I should have done it already," he says, his voice low and dangerous.

"Yes," I gasp, and the orgasm comes on fast and hot. I move my hips back against Graham until he holds me still, filling me while he curses.

"Do you have any idea how fucking hot you are?" He leans over me, covering me with his body. "Do you have any idea how bad I want you?"

I can't answer because I'm holding on for dear life.

Graham pushes in so deep he bottoms out and lets out a low grunt, and then he's finding his release as well.

He pulls out with a reluctant sigh, then gathers me onto his lap.

He tips his head back to rest on the chair. I kiss down the line of his neck to his collar and he makes a satisfied noise.

We stay like that for a long time, and then Graham offers me a shower and some clothes to borrow.

"Borrow?" I tease. "You want me to spend the night?"

"I don't want you going downstairs," he says, and guides me into the shower. "I didn't have you all week, stay with me tonight."

GRAHAM

I've never thought much about lying around in the bath before. Baths don't make money, and lying around doesn't, either.

But you couldn't pay me to get out of the bath with Maddie. It's fucking heaven.

Her wet hair drips onto my chest, and she curls her whole body up onto mine, and *fuck.* I don't care if I lose everything so long as I can hold on to this.

The air is filled with the scent of her shampoo and her body wash and the clean, warm smell of her skin, and part of me wants to save this memory somehow so I have it forever.

Maddie sighs, turning to kiss my collarbone.

"What's on your mind?" I ask, running my fingers through her hair. It's slippery from her conditioner and doesn't snag at all.

"Oh, it's nothing."

"Tell me anyway."

"I was just thinking about how content I am." She lifts her hand from the water and the sound is soothing. I take her hand in mine, enjoying the warmth as she settles into me.

I murmur and kiss the side of her neck, loving how her body reacts. "Is that right?"

"Yes. And..." She makes another soft sound. She's careful with her words. "I don't know how to feel about it. I always thought it would take more of a fight. That's what I was used to, before."

"Before?"

"When I was younger."

"You're young now."

Maddie presses her sweet body against mine, and that's almost the end of the conversation. "I mean before I met you. I always felt like I was fighting for something. I felt like... if I *wasn't* fighting and going after my goals, then it would definitely turn out wrong. And it did, with my ex. I stopped fighting, and everything went to shit."

I stiffen at the mere mention of men who had her before me.

We're both quiet for a minute.

"It's different with you," she admits. "I don't feel like I have to fight for everything."

I don't want her to fight for a damn thing. Not when she's mine. Tension builds in my shoulders and I bite back so much of what I want to say.

Instead, I lean down and kiss her, my heart aching. Because I want to be the person who gives her the world. I want to tell her that.

But something's stopping me.

Something says I shouldn't go that far, and shouldn't offer her that, because maybe I'm not the man she needs. And one day this is going to end. It's merely an arrangement. A negotiation that has an undefined timeline. She knows it. I know it. But neither of us says it out loud.

CHAPTER 12

MADDIE

It was too good to be true.

It's all I can think, and I nearly tell Suzette just that when she texts me and asks how it's going.

I should have known that the minute I started to settle into what I thought was a fresh start, it was too good to be true. But I wanted to see the best in it. Looking on the bright side is what got me through hard times.

Now it all feels like a joke.

The next Monday after Graham leaves me a note, everything goes wrong at work. The weekend was amazing. Easy and carefree. Sleeping in, having lazy morning sex, and then enjoying the benefits of the penthouse while Graham worked. But it came and went far too quickly.

First thing in the morning, dressed in a prim and proper skirt suit, I show up at the office ready to tackle the day, but the CEO is in a terrible mood. I've worked for men like Michael Davies before. When they're irritable, everyone walks on eggshells. It's not a comfortable feeling.

Some of the work we were doing at the assistant level was misfiled or submitted to the wrong person, and when he calls the three of us in for a meeting with his secretary, I know it isn't going to go well.

And it doesn't.

I didn't cause any of the trouble—my work was fine and that's determined—but the CEO isn't happy to let the other assistant's mistake go. My jaw drops. I've been here almost three months and other than a few moments where small comments were made here and there, it's been fine. It's been great even connecting the company to charities and sharing successful strategies. I don't work directly with the CEO though. And now I know there's no way I ever could. I sit through about three minutes of him *yelling* at her—actually yelling—before I can't stand it anymore.

Someone had to defend the poor girl. And then he's yelling at me. As it turns out, I'm the one who's leaving, because the CEO fires me on the spot. I leave the office with shaking hands and angry tears in my eyes and call Suzette.

"I'm really sorry," I tell her, the second the call connects. "It didn't work out."

"Maddie, what?" There's a rustling sound like she's moving the phone to her other hand. "What didn't work out?"

"The job. I just got fired for being unable to handle the pressure." I tell her the story, getting angrier with every word that comes out of my mouth. "I couldn't sit by and let it happen, so I'm done. I left the office. It's over."

"Okay. Maddie, this is fine. It's a setback, obviously, but it's not the end—"

"Maybe it should be." I toss my hand in the air, frustrated beyond belief. "Maybe I should get real with myself and stop pretending that a positive attitude can fix every situation. I was kidding myself when I thought I could stay in this apartment."

"I don't think—"

"And I was kidding myself if I thought that I could get involved with a man and keep it casual." Emotions sweep through me and every small negative thought I've had for the past two months tangle with themselves at the back of my throat.

Suzette doesn't say anything. I get to an intersection by a flower shop and look away from all the pastel blooms in the window. They look like flowers for a celebration, and there's nothing to celebrate today.

"Did something happen with Graham?" Suzette asks carefully.

"He took me to meet his friends."

"I thought that went well. You said it did."

"Well, no, it didn't, because now they all know me, and I don't understand why he'd want that. He didn't want to show up alone, and they were *too nice,* like he's actually interested in anything beyond being fuck buddies."

"I thought that's what you wanted."

"I did, at the beginning," I burst out. "It seemed like fun, at the beginning. But every time we're together, I just get more confused. He seems like he wants something real with me, but he never says so."

"And you want to be with him."

"I can't be with him. I shouldn't even be in that building."

"Because of the cost?"

"Because of the rent, and because..." I don't want him to notice that I got *fired.* Tears leak into the corner of my eyes. It's then I realize, I'm so embarrassed. I don't want him to start thinking of me as the woman who couldn't handle her own life. We'd turned it into a sexy game, and now, in the space of a day, it's not a game anymore. I don't understand why everything feels like it's crumbling all at once. "I just can't."

Suzette says all the right things a friend would, but I don't hear any of it. All I can think about is how I'm going to have to explain to a man like Graham, someone who works their ass off day in and night out, that I got fired because I couldn't keep my mouth shut. I confess to Suzette as I try to calm myself down. "I would have willingly quit if he hadn't fired me. After all of these years, I don't have a job." My breath catches and I try to pull myself together, I try to get my emotions to make sense. I don't have a passion like he does. The voice in the back of my head tells the truth. *I'm just not good enough for a man like him, for an apartment like that, for a life like this. I'm a fraud.* My phone beeps. Another call is coming in.

"I have to go," I tell Suzette.

"Call me later," she says, just before I answer the next call. "Hello?"

"It's me." Kenzie's voice wobbles, like she's been crying, and my stomach sinks. I close my eyes, pressing my back to a building as the city passes me by. This is the worst timing. I can barely exhale as she continues. "Listen. I know you just started a new job, but I need help. The loan company said they're going to start taking money from my paychecks, and I need all of it for the rent, so I need—"

"You'll have to move here, then. You'll have to just...I don't know, Kenzie. You'll have to come here, and we can figure something out."

"I can't do that. You *know* that. My whole life is in Chicago, and it's not like I can just rent a car—"

"I don't know what else to tell you!" I try my best not to raise my voice at my cousin, but my throat feels like I swallowed a rock and my eyes were burning *before* and there's just nothing I can do. "I got fired today, Kenzie! I got fired. I don't have any extra money. I have to take drastic measures myself, so the only way I can—"

"Mom's sick," Kenzie says, her voice cold.

"What?"

"My mom is sick. That's why I haven't asked her. That's why I'm always asking *you*. Do you even care?"

"Kenzie." I lean against a lamppost, taking deep breaths. "What do you mean she's sick?"

"She has cancer," she tells me, and my entire body goes cold.

"Oh my God. I'm so sorry."

"I am too," she says, and she's choked up.

"Why didn't you tell me this before?"

"Because she said not to tell anyone. It's treatable, just expensive. She's going to be okay. She will...but also because I wanted to handle it," she tells me. "I wanted to figure out a way to solve it on my own. And I couldn't, obviously, or I wouldn't be calling. But it's not like I can call *her* because she's dealing with so many medical bills that she might lose her house, too."

"I'm sorry," I say. A driver in traffic cuts across to the opposite lane, almost hitting another car, and horns blare. "I'm sorry, Kenzie."

It's not enough, just to apologize. I'm stick to my stomach at the thought that my aunt has been sick...and nobody told me.

They probably didn't tell me because I got a whole new life with Kevin and disappeared into it and thought my cousin needed to get *her* head together.

I guess she's not the only one.

"None of this is your fault," Kenzie says in a voice that tells me it *is* my fault, at least a little. "I know how hard you worked to get where you are. I just thought..." She lets out an angry sigh. "I thought you'd understand, because of that."

"Kenzie." I rub at my forehead with the back of my hand, blinking back tears. "I just need some time. I'll figure something out, I swear, I just can't do it right this minute. I haven't even gotten home from the office yet."

"No." She takes a deep breath, and I can almost see her straightening her back. "I'll figure this out. You deal with your stuff. I'll deal with mine."

"Kenzie, please—"

My cousin hangs up.

I don't blame her for how she feels. I couldn't possibly blame her for that when I've felt the same way so many times. But this, on top of getting fired, on top of thinking that I'd avoided disaster...

It's too much. I'm quick to text my aunt that I love her and miss her. I almost tell her I know but I don't. Instead I just let the tears out.

She answers back with a text telling me she misses me, and she hopes I'm living my big-city-life dreams and maybe one day she can come down to see me. I have to read it all through glassy eyes. We've never been a super close family, but I that doesn't mean I don't love them all.

I get back to my building and go through the lobby as fast as I can, my head down. If Graham is in here today, I don't want to see him. My phone buzzes with a text, but I don't look at it. I throw myself into the elevator.

It's empty and I shove myself into the corner of it.

The hall on the eighth floor is empty too, so nobody sees the tears start to fall as I fumble to get my key in the door.

I slam it behind me and kick off my shoes, drop my purse, and go for my clothes. I don't want to be in the skirt suit for another second.

"Don't feel sorry for yourself," I say out loud. "*Don't.*"

But I do. I feel sorry for myself, for my cousin, for my aunt. I feel sorry for my family that they have me to deal with.

My chest aches, my head hurts, and it's all gone wrong. *Again.*

In the bedroom, I fall on the bed and cry. The sheets and blankets Kevin and I picked out together feel awful, but they're the ones I have. At least they shelter me a little while I cry into the pillow.

It almost feels like the world got together and decided to put me in my place. Let's be honest, it's what I deserve. For so long, I wanted to believe that the world was on my side. It seemed too sad to think that we live in a universe that doesn't care what happens to us.

It's true, though. The universe doesn't care what happens to us. It doesn't care about anything, and no amount of finding the silver lining will change that.

My phone buzzes three more times, and finally I push it off the bed. It lands on the floor, muffled by the carpet. What does anybody want from me? They don't want to sit on the other end of the phone and listen to me cry about the mistakes I've made in my life, and they *don't* want to come over.

I don't want Graham to see me like this.

I don't want anybody to see me like this.

I don't even want to see myself like this.

Every time I think I've cried all of the feelings out, more tears come. It starts to seem like one long pattern. Everything went wrong before Kevin. It went wrong when I got cocky about my abilities in life. It went wrong when I thought I could come back from any breakup, any setback. It went wrong when I just kept pushing ahead into the next thing instead of taking stock of how I was causing all the trouble *myself.*

I don't know how long it's been when someone knocks at the door.

Shit. I didn't lock it. I closed it, but I didn't lock it, and now anybody could walk in.

Only I know that it's not going to be *anybody.* It's going to be Graham, coming to see me at my most pathetic. My stomach turns. He could fix all of this, but I'm done asking to be bailed out. I'm not going to sit up on the edge of the bed and tell him he can fuck me in exchange for fixing...

I don't know. All of it. Kenzie's situation, my situation, my aunt, the apartment.

And that might mean I can't enjoy *him* anymore. So it's not just all this bad news in one day, it's him, too.

He keeps knocking, and I don't say anything. My throat feels too rough to answer him. My body feels too heavy to get up and answer the door, much less push the covers off, so I just lie there.

He's going to leave, eventually. That's what always happens in the end. People want you for one thing, and the second you don't give them exactly that, they're gone.

I don't even blame him.

I'm the one who pushed for all this. I'm the one who thought it would be okay.

I keep waiting for Graham to leave and for the knocking to stop. Instead, after a while, I hear the door to my apartment open, then close.

It's quiet for a while longer, and then soft footsteps come toward the bedroom. He's passing the sitting area where we fucked the first time. I wonder if he thinks about it.

I hope I can stop thinking about it.

The bedroom door creaks a little on its hinges. Even the door is a sign that things aren't going how they should. Doors in an apartment like this shouldn't creak, which means I should have called maintenance to make sure the hinges were oiled or whatever, and I haven't done that.

It's a tiny failure, barely even a mistake, but it makes more tears leak out of my eyes. I try to wipe them away.

It doesn't do anything.

Graham steps into the bedroom and hovers near the door, his mouth a thin line. His shoulders are tense. He's obviously uncomfortable, and I didn't expect anything else. He didn't sign up for me crying in my bed because I got fired. He signed up for hot sex in exchange for the rent.

I sniffle into my pillow and try to get myself under control.

It doesn't work.

"Madelyn..." Graham says carefully. "Are you okay?"

There are lots of things I want to say to him, like, *please get into the bed with me.* Like, *could you explain how everything keeps going to shit when I try so hard.* Like, *what is it about me that makes it so impossible to keep anything good? Why aren't I just better? Why can't I just go along with what life wants from me?*

"No."

There's an even longer silence. I wait for him to leave without saying anything else, but Graham just stands there, watching.

"Should I come back another time?" he asks.

The answer is no. He shouldn't come back. He should go on with his life and forget the game we've been playing. Both of us should, because games like this only end in heartache, even if they're not the final cause of it.

But my heart hurts for how much I want to be touching him. If I were the strong woman I pretend to be, I could tell him the real truth—that it was a mistake to get involved with each other and the best thing we can do now is walk away gracefully.

I don't feel very strong at the moment. I feel weaker than I've ever felt, and I just can't give him up.

Not right now. What the hell am I supposed to do? Tell him I got fired, I failed my cousin, and my aunt is sick? No. No, I cannot and will not burden him with that when I don't even deserve him.

"Yes." I tell him. "Red." I tell him because I don't know what else to say. I just want him to know I'm not okay.

Graham takes a breath, and I can't tell if it's a disappointed noise or a relieved one. His hands come out of his pockets, and then he puts them back in.

"I'll leave you alone, then."

I nod, mostly into the pillow. My bedroom door opens again, and then it shuts.

My heart breaks.

It's more painful than being fired, more painful than my conversation with Kenzie, more painful than anything else. I can't breathe because it hurts too much.

I was hoping he would come to me. I was hoping he would see what a wreck I was and just make this feeling go away.

I was hoping he'd fallen in love with me, because I've fallen for him, even if I haven't been willing to admit it.

Graham is the only person I want comfort from right now, and I sent him away, and he just *went*.

That's the proof I needed and it hurts. I need to leave. I should have left when Kevin did and made my way somewhere else. I could've figured it out; I know that now. But leaving felt like giving up.

Well, sometimes it's better to give up. That's obviously a lesson I've learned too late. Somehow, I thought that if I had the apartment, I'd at least have *something* to prove myself, but I don't.

I have nothing.

I turn over and sob into the pillow until I fall asleep.

CHAPTER 13

GRAHAM

This is why I don't do relationships. Because what the fuck was that?

She's not well. I know she's not well. But she sends me away and...I fucking had to because of a goddamn word? I pace the entrance to my penthouse, staring at the security camera in her hall. *What the fuck even was that?*

I've never felt so inadequate.

I text her to tell me when she's available to talk and I get no response.

I text Brian to tell him what happened and ask what to do and all he can say is that sometimes women are emotional and to give her space.

That doesn't feel right. None of this feels right. But I have no experience in these matters. I don't know what the fuck happened, let alone what to do.

It keeps me awake all night. I can't sleep. I can't even lie down. I just keep staring at my phone, typing out messages and deleting them.

I've been a fool. I took her to meet my friends, but the problem is that I don't know any of *her* friends. There's nobody I can call to find out what happened. If I did, it would be overstepping a boundary. She already safeworded me. Legally I probably committed a crime entering her house like that. Maddie's never introduced me to any of her friends, she's only talked about a few people in passing. If she wanted me to meet them, she would have made that happen. I have to remind myself that what we have is an arrangement, and it's one she needs so she'll come back. She'll answer me when she's in better spirits and she'll tell me what happened. She has to, doesn't she?

Uncertainty washes through me and I feel like an even bigger prick assuming money will keep her coming back to me. *Fuck!*

All through the evening and then the next day she never texts me and never calls.

The only person who *does* call is Harland Porter.

He calls at one in the fucking morning, and when my phone rings, everything in me lights up. It's her. It's *her.*

But it's Harland goddamn Porter.

"What is it?" I snap, not caring if he doesn't like my tone.

"I've been up, just going through some things in my head, and I wanted to run them—"

"Harland, if you want to sell me the building, then sell the damn thing to me. If you don't want to, then stop stringing me along. I've had enough of this. You know where I stand. Make up your mind by tomorrow at five, or I'm pulling out."

That shocks him into silence. "Graham, I—"

"Tomorrow at five," I repeat, and hang up the call.

My entire body trembles as I sit back down and stare at the security cameras. I text Brian to ask how bad it may get if I were to go back down there. And foolishly I text Maddie again and she texts back that she needs to sleep.

Graham: *what happened?*

Maddie: *I need to get back to sleep.*

Graham: *you told me that but I need to know what happened.*

Maddie: *I can't right now. I just...I'm sorry.*

It's then that Brian texts me as well.

Brian: *Seriously. Just give her some time.*

I drop my phone, hating every fucking minute of this. Sometime after dawn I doze off on the couch in my living room and wake up again with a jolt at ten to nine.

Fuck me.

I'm usually in the office by now, but I feel wrecked from the night awake. Every single one of my muscles hurts like I've run a marathon. I stomp into my shower and let the hot water do its work. The steam surrounds me and my head races with every thought imaginable. The only conclusion I come to is that she's leaving. Something happened to pull her away. Was it her fucking ex? I don't know what I'll do if she's actually leaving me.

There are no messages from Harland Porter on my phone when I get out, but I don't care.

I don't *care*. What the hell was so important about this property? What was I trying to prove by sticking things out with a man who doesn't know what he wants? The only things that matter are Maddie and the fact that she didn't message me.

I shave at the sink, barely looking at myself. This is a horrible feeling. It's the feeling I've been resisting for years. I didn't want anything to be more important than making sure I had the right life, and I was wrong.

I was just wrong.

I tap the razor too hard on the edge of the sink and get a grip on myself.

I didn't know what to do for her because I've spent all this time worrying about buildings instead of people. I lost my parents, so I thought that was it. There was nothing else for me to concern myself with but building a legacy that surpassed them.

I'm the one who did this to myself, and now to Maddie.

Getting dressed feels worthless. None of this shit matters,

either. None of the custom suits or tailored shirts or expensive watches. What the fuck are they worth? When it comes down to it, I'll be alone because I don't know how to love anyone anymore. I don't let them close so they don't let me close.

And I've never wanted anything more in my life than to wipe her tears away and to make whatever it was that hurt Maddie vanish.

I was focused on the wrong damn things in the first place.

Once I've got my shirt buttoned up, I put my head in my hands and force myself to breathe.

No. This is not how I wanted things to go. If she's going to push me away, I need her to know that I don't want her to. I need her to know that I...that I... *fuck!*

I don't know what to do for the rest of the day. I pace around my apartment, waiting to see if she'll call.

Eventually, I'm ready to admit that I'm the one who has to choose what I'm going to do. I can't keep waiting. So I make the decision to go down to the lobby and check in with the doormen.

I need to reset my view of the property, of Maddie, and of my entire life.

The ground floor is the best place to start.

I dress, double check to make sure I have my phone and wallet, and head for the door. My penthouse feels empty without Maddie. It's always been too much space for one person, but I ignored that feeling because it was a status symbol. A man like me is *supposed* to have a penthouse. It's what's best. It's the crowning jewel. But what the fuck good is a king without his queen?

In reality, a man like me is supposed to know better. He should understand that he can't just waste away by himself, alone in his penthouse, counting piles of money that do fuck all to fill the gaping hole in his chest.

He should've known from the beginning that all the money would never be enough.

In the elevator, I lean against the wall and tell myself over and over again that it's not too late.

I don't even know what it's not too late for.

My phone rings as I'm stepping out of the elevator, and my heart pounds thinking it's her.

It isn't.

"Hey, Scott," I say into the phone, trying to hide my disappointment. "I'm on my way to the office."

"Oh, please. You can spare a couple minutes for me."

"Yeah."

"We need to get together again. What are your plans on Thursday? All my wife talks about is seeing you two again."

You two.

I go the opposite way from the lobby, following the hall without looking where I'm going until I find an alcove with a bench.

"I'm not sure I can make that happen."

"What?" Scott laughs, like I've made a hilarious joke. "We all want to see her again, and we're sick of seeing you twice a year."

"You see me twice a year because I'm busy."

"We're all busy," he argues, still laughing. "We can't let you slip away, man. That's how you lose people."

"I..." What am I supposed to say to that? Not having dinner together isn't how you *lose* people. They work themselves to death and die. That's how you lose them. And I don't think eating at fancy restaurants will do anything to stop that.

Except...he's right. I felt miserable last night because there was nobody to call. Nobody I wanted to talk to except Maddie. Because I've pulled myself away from all of them. "I know that."

"You okay?" His voice gets softer, and I can tell Scott's catching on to the fact that he got me at a bad time.

I almost lie out of habit. That's what I've done all this time. There's no reason to burden anyone else.

Then I think of Maddie, crying in her bed.

"I don't know." Unwanted emotions surface and I pinch the bridge of my nose.

"What happened?" There's a *creak* in the background of the call, like he's sat down behind his desk. A door closes somewhere nearby. Scott didn't call me to listen to me complain about my own foolish mistakes, but somewhere in the city, he's sitting down, ready to listen.

"I don't know." I feel sick from how little I know. From

how little I asked. From how unwilling she was to confide in me. "Something's going on with Maddie."

"Oh," he says, thoughtful. "And she didn't tell you what it was?"

"No." I don't know how much to tell him. It's not really my business, what's happening in Maddie's life, only...it *is* my fucking business. I care about her, and I'm not going to stop because something happened that I wasn't there to prevent. "I went up to see her last night, and she was crying. Told me she wanted me to leave."

"And have you talked today?"

"No."

"This was last night?"

"Yeah."

"Jesus, Graham. Go knock on her door."

"I don't think she wants that."

"You're her boyfriend. I'm sure she wants that. Even if she doesn't want to lean on you, she wants to lean on you. Trust me."

This is the worst possible time to admit that I lied about all the details I gave my friends. "We didn't meet at the bar. We met at the building."

Scott lets out a surprised laugh. "At your building, you mean?"

"She lives here. And she fell behind on the rent, so..."

"So you swooped in to be her hero?"

God I love his version so much better. Her hero. I roll my eyes and know damn well I took advantage. If only he knew how much I wanted to tell him that story. If only he knew how much I wanted it to be true.

"In a way."

"Um...what *kind* of way?"

"The kind where she told me she'd do anything if I could help her out with the rent, and I agreed."

He doesn't say anything.

I check my phone.

Call's still connected.

"Scott?"

"You made a deal with her for sex?"

"It sounds terrible when you say it like that."

"I'm not judging." I think he might not be. Scott's always been the most levelheaded of us all. I can hear him drumming his fingertips on the desk in a slow rhythm. "She was into it, I'm assuming, since—"

"Yes, she was *into* it," I snap. "I wouldn't have done it otherwise. You know that."

"I do," he says quickly. "I do. Then what happened? You decided to date her?"

"The arrangement continued in a way where we became closer and there are feelings...at least on my end."

"Okay," he says slowly and appears to be more agreeable with the situation. "But...it's nothing formal."

"We're not boyfriend and girlfriend," I say, hating how cynical it sounds and how petulant the statement is.

"You might want to have a conversation about that, if... things are happening."

"Yeah."

A minute passes. It starts to seem like a good idea. To tell her that I'm her boyfriend now and that she can confide in me for more emotional things. I shift where I stand, thinking it's not going to work, but if she's going to leave me, it's an offer. I don't know what it's worth, but it may be worth something.

Scott just waits on the other end of the line.

"Graham."

"Yeah?"

"Go talk to her. You're not going to fuck up your life by telling someone you love them."

"I didn't say that."

"You didn't have to," he answers, and I let that sink in. "Go talk to her. Text me tomorrow. We're all going to come to your office and drag you out kicking and screaming if that's what we have to do."

"Don't or I'll send building security after you," I attempt to joke although it doesn't make me feel any better.

"I can take your security," he says comically and hangs up.

I'm left standing there in the alcove next to the bench, wondering if Scott's right or if I'm right or if nobody's going to be able to tell until I find Maddie and talk to her.

Although doubt creeps in, I'm almost certain she feels for me a hint of what I feel for her.

Before I can head back up, the lobby doors open and a gust of air comes through, as does Madelyn, the woman who's tempted me to want more in this life.

When the hell did she leave? The question answers itself as I remember I dozed off earlier. I swallow thickly, feeling even less than worthy.

The sight of her is like a punch to the chest. She's wearing a gorgeous pink dress that looks like a dream and large sunglasses, probably meant to hide how long she spent crying yesterday. Maddie stops when she sees me, hesitates, then continues on toward the elevator.

I don't say a word, instead I step out to meet her in the middle of the floor. Maddie lets out a breath and we continue walking. I settle in beside her and we go toward the elevators.

Privacy will be good for this. My hands go numb as she doesn't make a move to touch me, to kiss me. I think she's really going to fucking end it with me and the thought won't leave me alone.

She can't. The only thing I know is that if she plans to leave, I have to tell her I love her. I can't let her leave me without knowing that she means more to me than our arrangement.

She takes one look at the silver doors and keeps going past, finally stopping at the same alcove I just took that call in. Maddie turns to face me. One more deep breath, and she pushes the sunglasses up to the top of her head.

I was right. Her eyes are all red, her cheeks are blotchy, and she looks like she needs a hug.

"Hi," she says.

"Madelyn."

At the sound of my voice, she closes her eyes. After a beat, she opens them again. "I'm glad I saw you down here, because I...I wanted to give my notice."

Fuck, no. "Your notice?"

"I wanted to ask you if I could end my lease early. I know that's technically not what's in the contract, but I've considered all my options, and I need to move somewhere that's...within my means."

What the hell is she talking about? We have an arrangement. She could live here for the rest of her life and still be well within her rent budget.

"I can take on whatever bills you need," I offer her. "Credit cards or whatever it may be. Simply give them to me."

"No," she says, and her chest rises with a stutter.

"Why?" I'm not proud of how I sound in the moment, and I can't help stepping closer, my chest aching. "Should I have stayed last night?"

Maddie looks down and away, slowly dragging her eyes back to mine. "It's not that."

I can't let her do this. I can't let her disappear out of my life. I can't spend from now until I die thinking about her.

"I should have stayed last night," I tell her, taking charge of the conversation. At least *my* part of the conversation. "That was a bad move, to leave you alone like that. I could have stayed in the living room, given you space, but been there." I think out loud, attempting to learn from my mistake. "I am not well versed in..." I swallow, not knowing what to call what we have given the circumstances. "Let me make it up to you."

"Graham, I don't—"

"Come to dinner. Have something to eat, and we can talk." My voice is even, my suggestion strong yet gentle. So at odds with the chaos and loss that run like wildfire through my blood.

She presses her lips together, and I'd give just about anything to kiss her.

Red. The word hasn't been said in this moment, but it was before and it lingers between us. "It'll be all right," I tell her. "Whatever it is, whatever you need," I remind her, "I will take care of you."

But she's on edge, tensing up, and I don't want to push her until we've had a chance to lay everything out on the table.

"Are you hungry?" I ask.

Maddie runs a hand through her hair, almost knocking her glasses off in the process. "I haven't eaten much," she admits. "Yes. I'm hungry."

"Then come to dinner. Or just...come upstairs. I can have dinner brought to us."

She hesitates one more time, and I offer her my arm.

"It's not far," I tell her, keeping my voice light. "Only an elevator ride away." At this moment I remember the first time I laid eyes on her. I can't lose her. I did once before, and I don't know what will come of me now that I know every little bit about her that I do. "I don't want to lose you," I confess to her, and her eyes meet mine with surprise and maybe hope.

"Okay," she says softly, and takes my arm.

Thank fuck. I at least have a chance.

CHAPTER 14

MADDIE

I have a slight headache from crying most of the night, and I don't feel like I look my best, but Graham doesn't say a word about it as he whisks me upstairs to the penthouse.

The first thing he does is put me on the couch in the living room and hand me a bottle of water. I take sips from it while he moves around the apartment.

He's tense and I feel awful for all of this. I don't know how it got to this point. I was living a fairy tale that wasn't meant for me. I'm so sorry I dragged him into this.

"Are you drawing a bath?" That's definitely the sound of running water.

Graham doesn't answer. He returns a few minutes later with a stack of clothes in hand. A robe—new and silky—along with a comfortable outfit that could easily be pajamas or the classier version of loungewear.

"You had these laying around?" I ask as he hands me the folded bundle.

"Maybe," he says. "Why don't you get changed? If we're not going out, then you're allowed to be comfortable."

"Get changed or have a bath?"

"Either. Both. Whatever will get you to talk to me."

When we get to the main bathroom, the tub is filled, a candle flickers on the edge, and there's a small glass of wine balanced on a tray that stretches over the water.

It's far too romantic for what I feel like I deserve. I've messed this up. Just like I messed everything else up.

"Are those *rose petals*?" I can't help a soft smile of disbelief at the crimson petals floating on the surface. "Did you put rose petals in the bathwater?"

"I told you I'd make it up to you."

Graham bustles toward the door. "The remote on the tray connects to the sound system. It'll play whatever you want, just scroll through the screen for the options."

He's drawn a *bath* for me.

"If you don't want to talk, we can listen to music."

I put the clothes on the towel shelf and look down at the steaming hot water. It looks like heaven although I may fall asleep in it, I'm so damn tired.

"Where did you get rose petals?" I whisper, and then

decide to take him up on it.

The wine's sweet and chilled, the water's hot and soothing, and the music brings it all together. I expect him to follow me in, but when I sink fully in, he isn't there.

The music is quiet enough that I can hear him moving around in the penthouse. A door opens and shuts. Low voices talk to one another. I watch the rose petals float across the surface of the tub. I feel awful for last night.

It's all on the tip of my tongue. I didn't really want him to go. I just didn't know what else to say. I just wanted it all to stop.

With both hands, I splash the water on my face and attempt to just calm down. Suzette's advice echoes in my head: calm down. Tell him when you're calm.

She said it will be okay, but I don't see how any of this is going to be okay.

I sip the wine until it's gone and let the heat of the water take some of the ache out of my muscles. Whew. A girl really shouldn't cry that hard if she doesn't want to feel like crap all day.

When I've soaked up all the relaxation I can, he still isn't in the tub.

I get out and dry off with one of Graham's ridiculously fluffy towels. His initials are monogrammed on them in dark blue, like his stationery, and that makes me feel lighter for some reason. I think I just like the sight of his initials.

There's an arrangement of glass dispensers on the counter

with lotion that has the light scent of aloe, and I spend some time rubbing it into my skin, waiting for him, before I change into the clothes he's brought.

He *must* have had them here. But I don't think he bought them today.

Did he have them here for me all along?

Did he want to ask me to stay and make it clear that he has everything I need?

I look much better in the mirror when I'm finished with the lotion. Last night was rough, and it showed on my face, but now my cheeks are pink from the bath and my eyes aren't as red as they were. You can hardly tell I was crying.

I slip the robe over my shoulders, tie the belt in front, and go back out into the main penthouse, quietly, but not without calling out his name.

He doesn't answer so I call out louder, "Graham?"

There's music playing in the living room, and someone has set up a table with a white tablecloth in front of the floor-to-ceiling windows. Graham's lighting a candle in the center as I pad up behind him.

I have to blink away the disbelief.

"You shouldn't have done all this," I say, more heat flooding my face. "After last night—"

"Yes, I should because I want to." He finishes lighting the candle and smiles at me. "And because I want *you*." It's a shy, vulnerable smile, and he leans forward to kiss my forehead before he pulls out my chair and helps me into it.

Graham has unbuttoned the top two buttons of his shirt and rolled the sleeves up to his elbows, so I'm not the only one who's made themselves more comfortable.

My mouth waters, looking at his forearms. There's a deep need and a deep ache at the thought of lying in his arms.

It's all I want. He pulls the chair out for me and I thank him, once again taken aback.

I have a feeling though that he really wants to talk, and I know I have a lot of explaining to do.

I focus on the table instead. He's put two flowers in a vase near the edge of the table and they're lovely. I was *not* in a good place when I saw that flower shop yesterday. I love flowers, and I happen to believe that beautiful flowers can make any bad situation at least a little better.

I almost start to admit how foolish I feel. How I'm just emotional because of my cousin, because of my aunt, and because of money and this situation and all of my uncertainty. I nearly let all the words tumble out, but when I look up, Graham has an expression I can't place, and I keep my lips firmly shut.

Graham steps away from the table, returning a minute later with the bottle of wine. He hesitates over my glass. "Did you like it?"

"I loved it." I give him a smile I know doesn't reach my eyes, and he smiles back. He's a striking man, and his charming look sends heat all through me.

Graham pours us both a glass, then leaves again.

It's quiet but for the gentle classic music. With steadying breaths I prepare to just come clean and tell him I'm in over my head in more ways than one.

He comes back with plates that go on top of the fancy china at our places, then leaves one more time. By the time he's done bringing the food, we have a basket of hot, fluffy rolls, a silver dish of mashed potatoes that look like they're to die for, two more sides, a plate of seared scallops and lobster tails, and a plate of very tender beef that almost looks like stew. All I know is that it smells like heaven, and I hadn't realized how hungry I was.

Graham takes his place across from me and scans the table. "Is there anything else I can get for you?"

You, I want to say but instead opt for gratitude. "No. This looks amazing. Thank you."

We eat for a few minutes. I was right. The mashed potatoes *are* to die for. Everything is swimming in butter and just the right amount of salty goodness. Graham looks even more handsome with the candlelight on his face.

We eat, although I eat slowly. I'm certain I know what comes next and I'm not ready.

It's still too silent and I know it is when he clears his throat. "I wanted to talk to you about last night," he says tentatively.

"Are you sure we should...now?" I nearly chicken out.

"I think we should. I'm sorry I didn't stay to talk longer." Graham looks me in the eye, his regret clear. "I mean it, Maddie."

"I'm sorry I said that word."

His silverware stops in midair. "I'm sorry I listened to it," he tells me. "I know that's wrong but leaving you because you safeworded me isn't what—"

"I didn't want you to leave. I just wanted it to stop."

He stops and I apologize for interrupting.

"Did you not think I'd leave?"

"I thought you wouldn't push for what was wrong," I tell him.

He drops his silverware. "Did you want me to stay?" he asks.

"I wouldn't have pushed you away if you'd come to bed." I almost tell him I'd rather he have taken me to his bed though.

His jaw clenches and he drops his silverware to his plate for a drink of wine.

"I only left because I thought that's what you wanted," he tells me when he puts the glass down. "No, not what you wanted. I left because when you say red, it means it stops, which means I leave."

"No. You didn't have to leave." I'm quick to correct him.

He pauses, his eyes boring into mine. "Don't use that word again unless it's because of something sex related Madelyn. Even if you want me to leave." He's deathly serious and I nod and tell him I won't use it if it's not about something in the bedroom.

He's more tense and starts to say something but then stops.

"I'm sorry. I didn't know you would think I meant for you to leave. I just didn't know what to say, I didn't want to say what I was thinking, but I didn't want to be alone."

"Are you all right?" he asks me when tears prick my eyes.

I swallow, thinking about how badly I've messed this up, about how I lost my job, thinking about my cousin and how she can't rely on me, and about my aunt. "I don't think so."

"I'd like to know what made you so upset, if you're willing to share it."

"I don't know where to start," I admit.

"Start from the beginning."

"I got bad news yesterday. A lot of it actually."

"What kind of bad news?" he asks, his elbows on the table, his hands folded under his chin, entirely focused on me.

I want to tell him. I want him to know everything. I don't care if he fixes it or not, I just want him to know. I don't know what's going to happen between us, but I do know that if I don't tell him, I'll wonder what he would have said. I'll wonder what would have happened after this moment.

"Well. It turns out that my boss is an asshole. *Was* an asshole, I mean." I dab the corner of my eyes.

His forehead furrows. "Was?"

"I mean..." I wave my wine glass at him. "He didn't die.

He's just not my boss anymore. I got fired because I told him to stop yelling at one of the other assistants. It was…" It hits me, maybe for the first time, how silly that whole thing was. Why would I have wanted to work there, anyway? I'd have come to that conclusion sooner or later, and I'd have had to find another job. "It was just not a good situation. But I worked so hard to get the job in the first place that it felt like a total disaster."

"Anyone would be upset about that."

"That's not all." I let out a sigh and a frown deepens in my expression. "My cousin called on the way home with more bad news."

Graham stays quiet and patient.

"She's struggled with student loans for a long time. I love her so much, and I've always done all I can to help her, but when my ex left, I couldn't help and it really screwed her over. She can't afford it on her own and I told her I'd be there for her. I promised her because I thought…well because I didn't know my fiancé was cheating on me. I thought that if I could get a job, I'd be in a position to make things easier. But she called yesterday, just after I'd been let go, and I snapped at her. I told her to figure it out for herself."

"I'm sure, given time…she can't blame you for that."

"Well, she also told me that my aunt is sick." This is the part that feels the worst to talk, or think, about. "I called her today. Complications from cancer treatment. I spent the night texting her and then my aunt. It's treatable but...they can't afford it. She can't get the medicine she needs because she has so much medical debt already, and insurance is a nightmare, and..."

He looks across the table at me, nothing but concern in his face. My first thought it that I hope he doesn't think I'm lying. That I'm trying to use him. "I want you to know that I don't expect anything from you. This isn't..." Tears blur my eyes at the thought of him thinking I would lie to him. That I would use him for money. "This is exactly why I couldn't..." I start to say and his chair groans against the floor as he pushes it out to come to me. He sits closer, his arm around me and telling me it's all right. All the while I'm falling to rubbish all over again.

"I know I couldn't have fixed all of it, but yesterday, it felt like I couldn't fix anything. And I wanted to. That's why I was so upset. Then, when you came to my apartment, I was..."

Graham presses his lips together, like he's stopping himself from interrupting.

"I was ashamed," I finally manage. "I was ashamed to let you see me like that. Because in the beginning of all this, I felt like our deal was giving me a little control over my life."

"I understand."

"Do you? And I was ashamed because I already feel like I'm using you."

"How could you possibly be using me?" he asks.

"For the money...like degrading myself for—"

"Do you find being with me degrading?" he cuts me off to ask.

My face gets twice as hot. "No. I don't. I liked what we did together, and even more than that, I liked spending time with you. Your friends...I was so happy to meet your friends. That meant a lot to me."

"But?"

"But when I got fired, all I could think is that you're going to think less of me. That..." I can't even get the words out because they all scream in my head telling me to shut up and that I'm making it worse. And that I'm going to lose him.

"I don't want you to think I'm coming to you because I'm desperate and need money."

Graham's quiet for a minute, looking down at his plate. Then he looks back up at me.

"What I spend my money on is my choice. And if I want to give it all to you, that is for me to concern myself with, not you."

"It doesn't change that I was scared you'd think a certain way or that..." It takes me a minute to find my voice. "I thought I was losing you, too. I just thought that you wouldn't want to keep doing that when it was clear I didn't have another option and that I was hard on money."

"Did you have another option when we started?" He asks in his logical sensical way.

"No," I say slowly. "But my feelings weren't as complicated."

He nods as if he understands, and my heart pounds.

"Okay." Graham takes out his phone. "First off, I'm going to take care of these problems."

"Which problems?" I feel sick. I don't want him to think for one second that I only want his money.

"All of them."

"Graham, I don't want your—"

"I would like it if you would allow me to do what makes me happy, my little temptress." He holds my gaze and then gives me an asymmetrical smile. "Let me do this simply because I want to."

"I want you because I want you," I tell him and hope he believes it.

"And I want you because I want you," he responds, and I do believe it. I believe him. This time when tears prick they're for a different reason, but I push the emotions down.

"And as for your job—"

"You can't get me my job back."

"You don't want that job back," he says simply, and he's right. "But if you want to search for one, I will help however I can. And if you don't want one and want to go back to charity work, I will help however I can there as well."

"You're too good to me," I whisper and there's a voice so loud begging me to tell him that I love him. That this is more to me than what we said it was.

"I'm fixing it," he says, steel in his eyes. "Tell me about

the loan companies. Do you have the information, or is there someone I need to call to get it?"

"I...I have all the information. I've been helping Kenzie with these for years." I manage to get up out of my seat and get my phone, then scroll through my inbox until I've found the ones with the account numbers.

Graham is still seated next to me and he sees. He takes his own phone out rather than taking mine. He doesn't dial the number of the service department at the student loan servicer. He calls the president of the company, at home, after business hours. He tells me to eat, kissing my forehead before disappearing into the back office.

How could I possibly eat? I push the food around on the plate praying, all the while hoping, I can text my cousin that she doesn't have to worry any longer. She only moved out there because I convinced her to follow her dreams. I set her up for failure like I did myself. If Graham can fix this, I will owe him more than just a blow job or anal.

Kenzie's loans are gone in less than twenty minutes, vanished into thin air.

Then he moves on to my aunt's medical bills. That takes closer to thirty minutes, because some of the bills have gone into collections.

Those are gone before I can finish my glass of wine. I'm practically dizzy with disbelief. I know he's wealthy. Wealthier than my ex and wealthier than most. But I didn't realize just how much money he had.

I can't stop thanking him and I don't even know how to tell Kenzie or my aunt.

"I told you this would be easy for me to do and that I wanted to do it."

Finally, Graham puts his phone face down on the table, and I put mine down, too. It's like the weight of the world has been lifted off my shoulders. I've been worrying about my cousin for so long that I can't remember what it's like *not* to worry about her.

"Graham, I don't know how I could ever repay you."

"I'm not asking you to," he tells me, and my gaze drops to my plate. I'm grateful but I also feel so inadequate.

"I wish there was something I could do," I finally manage.

"I will settle for you telling me that you will spend this week with me in this apartment and you will keep me company."

"For just this week?"

"For this week, in my penthouse. Not going to your apartment," he adds as if that stipulation would make the deal somehow harder to accept.

"Just be with you...for the week?" I ask him.

"Just be with me," he answers, and I take a steadying inhale.

"I would stay with you regardless."

"And I would pay those bills regardless as well. So we can call it even."

My bottom lip drops slightly and I remind myself that

this is real life. That this man I have fallen for is better than any dream. He is more than any picture-perfect catalog man I could have sold my soul to Satan for.

"You know you're my hero don't you?" I whisper, my fingers playing with the stem of the glass.

"You don't know how happy that makes me to hear. Madelyn, I am fairly certain I..."

My shoulders straighten at his hesitation, "You what?"

"That I...have caught feelings for you."

"I don't know what you mean," I whisper not because I don't, but because I don't believe he's saying it. Is he says he loves me?

"Yes, you do." His face has never looked so open. "It was never just sex for me. I don't care about your rent money. I don't care about any problem you could ever have with money. I don't care how much you need, or how much you want."

He pauses, and my heart beats faster. "What do you care about, then?"

"I care about being with you," he says. "So be with me. Stay with me. That's all I want."

"Do you love me, Graham?" I ask him cautiously, my heart beating wildly.

"I think I've loved you since the first moment I saw you, my little temptress."

The world moves slower as if something perfect has just slipped into place and all I can do is look him in the eyes and tell him the truth. "I love you too."

CHAPTER 15

GRAHAM
ONE MONTH LATER

I made sure to book dinner at the same restaurant we went to before. Afterall, last time went wonderfully and I know it impressed my Madelyn. Only this time my friends have reserved a larger table.

We have more two guests this time.

I flew in Maddie's aunt and cousin, and they stood in the airport lobby and hugged her and cried for almost ten minutes straight. It was the most touching thing I've ever seen, although incredibly uncomfortable to be surrounded by three crying women.

It was the least I could do given everything I've been told.

It's easy to see the family resemblance in all their faces. Some of that resemblance is down to relief, I think. From what Maddie explained, they've been going through a hard time for years.

It makes my chest ache to see them sitting at the table, eyes bright and smiling, because I never got to do this for my parents. Paying it forward to Maddie's family is the next best thing. There's no point in everything I've worked for and everything I've built if there's no one to share it with. It's all I can think as they chat away, sharing stories and telling me all about Madelyn as a little girl. The drive is easy, and I imagine the weekend is going to go exactly as I planned.

"We couldn't get you to bring a date ever and then you bring one and now three," Brian jokes as we walk in. Hugs are given all around and the four of us sit at the far end of the table.

After introductions, appetizers, and small talk, the conversation turns to us. To Madelyn and me.

Kenzie asks, her eyes shining as she looks at her cousin. "Did you know he was going to fall in love with you when you first kissed him?"

Maddie hesitates, her nose wrinkling with an adorable grin. I know she's going to say *no*. She couldn't have known anything. And that first kiss, that first night...it was a one-time reckless thing that could have ruined everything.

"You know what?" The table has fallen silent, and all my friends—my family—are waiting for her answer. "I think I might have felt that. But that was the first time I saw him, not when we..." She lets the sentence remain unfinished.

"What?" Julie says, truly curious. "The first time you saw him? When was that?"

"In an elevator." Maddie leans farther into my arm with a little shake of her head. "I was coming home from a dinner with my...well, with my ex-fiancé. He had proposed, and it was supposed to be one of the happiest days of my life."

Scott looks at me with wide eyes from his side of the table.

I mouth *shut up* at him.

"And I was happy." Maddie sounds thoughtful, like it was decades ago that I first saw her in that elevator. "I was excited, but...something was off about it. I was trying to convince myself that both of us were tired from the evening, and that's why he...I don't know. I just knew something wasn't right."

"He was such a fucking dick," Kenzie says quietly and her mother scolds her, smacking her gently with the cloth napkin.

"He wasn't the best," Maddie agrees. "So we were going up to the eighth floor, and the elevator stopped and then the doors opened, and Graham got on."

"Oooh," Julie says, then covers her mouth with her hands. "This is getting scandalous." I clear my throat and ignore her innocence.

"I just..." Maddie wriggles her shoulders a little. "I felt it. I felt *something,* looking at him, and I was barely even looking. I was mostly looking at him in the reflection on the doors. It probably seems crazy, but when his elbow touched mine, I—"

"Fell head over heels for him?" Scott asks.

"Yeah sure, something like that," Maddie says shrugging it off, and everybody at the table laughs.

"That's a fairy tale," Julie says, her fingers linked under her chin. "That's true love at first sight."

Maddie's eyes shine. "Yeah, I think it might have been."

I thought about Maddie for six long months after that single elevator ride. I'm not the kind of man who puts a lot of stock in fate and destiny, but when she opened the door to her apartment—when it was *her* and not some random woman I'd never seen before—I knew that was my chance. You don't get many second chances in life.

I couldn't admit it to myself at the time, but I'd have gone for her, fiancé or not. I might have tried to put it off and deny what I felt, but it wouldn't have lasted. There was something in that moment, trapped in that elevator with her, that changed me. Some piece of her fit perfectly with some piece of me, and I would have forever felt I was missing something if I hadn't found her again.

Dinner is served and the conversation at the table moves on to Kenzie's new classes. I set her up with an academic counselor in Chicago who was able to piece together her unfinished degrees and come up with a plan to finish both of them in two semesters. She talks about her projects and the inspiration she feels when she attends classes and how she's already made strong connections with several professors, which will come in handy when she goes job hunting. Just listening to her talk about all of her plans and how optimistic she is and how ready to take on the world she is…I know every penny was worth it.

Her aunt is doing very well, too. The medical bills had been a crushing weight on her, making it hard to recover from her treatments. Now that they're gone, Maddie says she's doing better than ever. She gets teary whenever she gets good news from her aunt.

And, just to make sure there are no more nasty surprises when it comes to hospitals, I've gone behind the scenes and made sure Maddie's aunt will never be turned away from any specialist she needs. She's not to see a single bill.

It's almost hard to imagine this table without Maddie. Her cousin fits here. Her aunt fits here. It's like they've always belonged here. I just didn't know anyone was missing.

It's tempting to bask in it for the rest of the evening. It wouldn't be so bad if we all just enjoyed ourselves without a big surprise event.

But what's the fun in that, if you have the most important question of your life to ask?

The conversation flows easily, with lots of laughter and inside jokes and explanations so that nobody's left out.

"Graham," Julie asks. "I was going to ask you. Did you close on that property?"

"Of course I closed on the property." I flash a smile across the table at her. "Did you think I gave up?"

"I heard things got a little dicey at the end."

"Harlan just needed some...strong encouragement."

He'd signed the contract to sell me the property while I was taking care of Kenzie's medical bills. The signed document showed up in my email, and he's been a delight to work with ever since.

I tell them, already looking forward to the new penthouse my little temptress is helping design, "Renovations on the building start next week, and it's going to be incredible when it's done." Turns out she has a passion for interior design and spending my money. Both of which are suiting her well and I'm enjoying it just as much as she is.

It's only when the night is coming to a close that I feel the nerves pick up. The waiters come in to take the dinner dishes away in preparation for coffee and dessert, and the conversation naturally lulls as they lean in, stacking plates and silverware and whisking it all away.

When they straighten up again, I pick up my drink and stand.

With a steadying breath, then another, I take in my friends who exchange meaningful looks with each other. I want to tell them all to cool it, to *relax,* but I can't say anything. Maddie looks up at me, her doe eyes bright with anticipation. She glances over at my friends with raised eyebrows, like they might give her some clue about what's going to happen, but they just look back at her with equally excited expressions.

"Madelyn," I start and stare into her eyes even as her mouth drops open. "From the first moment I saw you, I couldn't get you out of my head." Both of her hands cover her mouth and her eyes turn glassy.

Kenzie squeals, and Madelyn's aunt shushes her. Out of the corner of my eye, I can see them gripping each other's hands.

"I thought about you every day for six months after I got out of that elevator. The second I stepped out, I regretted doing it. I wanted to know more about you, and somewhere deep down, I knew there was something there I needed in my life."

Maddie's eyes shine with tears.

"I have to be completely honest with you. I've never been happier that someone couldn't pay the rent."

Affectionate laughter goes up around the table.

"I've told you this before, and I'll tell the entire world. There has never been anyone who made me feel what I feel for you. I wanted to be near you anyway I could. I still want to be with you in any way that I can."

Maddie keeps her eyes on me, and I want to remember her like this forever. She's pleased and content and in love, and I can't believe it took me so much of my life to look for this.

Then again, maybe it took me so long because she had to be in the right place at the right time.

Fine. Maybe I am the kind of man who believes in fate and destiny. I'll believe in anything that brought Maddie to me. My only wish is that my parents were here to see that I found someone like her. Someone to share my life with. Someone to help me through the dark times. Someone I can help through the dark times. I think somewhere, somehow, they know.

"I love you," I say and bend down on one knee, pulling the ring out of my pocket and presenting the diamond to her. "I want to spend the rest of our lives together so I can take care of you, make you happy, and be your husband. Will you marry me?"

She stands up out of her seat, tears running down her cheeks, throws her arms around my neck, and kisses me.

We're instantly surrounded by cheers. Her lips on mine is everything I need.

"Is that a yes, then?" Kenzie shouts and only then does she pull back from the kiss and looks me in the eyes.

Technically, she hasn't said *yes* yet. Not with her words. Technically, these are the last moments she'll spend as my girlfriend instead of my fiancée.

They're absolutely beautiful.

And what's to come is going to be *stunning*. I can't wait for all of it. Marrying her. Loving her forever. Being by her side for as long as I can.

I couldn't have earned a better deal than that if I worked every single minute for the rest of my life. I can only accept her for the gift that she is.

My Madelyn leans in, her lips close to mine, gives me a light kiss that feels like a promise, and whispers. "Yes."

Epilogue

Graham

The door opens and it's her. The woman from the elevator.

Same dark hair. Same dark eyes.

And now I know that it's her voice I like.

My head turns foggy with all the thoughts I've had of her for the last two months as she invites me into her apartment.

The scent of her in the air is the same, if a bit more subtle, and for a few seconds she's all I can see.

My gaze instantly flies to the rest of the room. Expecting to see the man on the lease. Expecting to see the man she was with in the elevator.

The door closes and the place is silent. She's all by herself, petite and gorgeous. And seemingly nervous.

The way she spoke on the phone says she needs something,

and it's likely on her boyfriend's behalf, too.

Her husband's.

Whoever he is.

The flush in her cheeks and her wide eyes are all the confirmation I need that she recognizes me, too. Her breathing quickens.

It takes great effort to keep my gaze on her eyes and not lower it. That's...not a thought I should ever have about a woman who lives here with someone else. A woman who hasn't been thinking about me as I have her, I'm sure.

I have the thought anyway. What the hell can anybody expect me to do? She's gorgeous, and she needs *something*.

And, from the look on her face, she's glad to see me.

She shakes her head, recovering. "Oh! We've met before. Or...I saw you in the elevator before."

I flash her an even and professional smile, and she smiles back in response, looking even lovelier than she did before. Then I offer her my hand. "Graham Maxwell."

She takes it, her hand feeling small and delicate in mine, but her touch is electric. It's exactly as it was when I brushed against her in the elevator. I shouldn't have felt anything.

"Maddie." She looks down at our hands and swallows, then drops her hand. "Please. Come in. Can I offer you anything to drink?"

"I think we'd better cut to the chase." Because if I have to stand here with her, looking at her, drinking her in, I'm going to do something foolish. "On the phone, you said you had an...urgent problem to discuss."

Her blush gets deeper and that color on her...fate is tempting me to be a lesser man. "Let's sit down. Is that okay?"

She could ask me for anything right now, and fiancé or not, husband or not, I'd give it to her. I can't explain why. I just know that it would feel absolutely right. "Lead the way."

She takes me through the apartment. It's done in understated neutrals with pops of color in the furniture and throw pillows. Maddie gestures toward a sitting area by the picture window in the living room. From here, we can see a long stretch of the city. It's an expensive view, and it's worth every penny. She lowers herself gracefully into a loveseat. I take an armchair across from her.

Maddie watches me.

"The emergency," I prompt.

She sits up straight, her chin coming up like she's about to go into battle. "Right. Yes. First, I wanted to apologize for the inconvenience. I know you're very busy."

"It's nothing. Tell me what's wrong."

Tell me what's wrong so I can fix it. There's no reason I should feel this drawn to a woman who's already taken. I need to get the hell out of here as quickly as I can. She's nothing but a temptress.

"I'd like to speak to you about the rent."

That's...not what I expected her to say.

"The rent for this apartment?"

"I'm sure, in a place like this..." She bites at her lip, fumbling for her next words. "I know you're probably not the one people come to about problems like this, but it's the weekend. I was up all night."

She sure as hell doesn't look like she was up all night. Maddie Cunnigham looks like she floated down from a cloud in heaven after a perfect night's sleep. The only sign that anything's wrong is the worry in her eyes.

"What's the problem with the rent?" I ask.

"I can't pay it. I can't pay all of it. This is my home, it's the only thing I have right now, and I can't quite cover the rent for this month."

Her breath comes shorter, and it all makes sense, how urgent she was on the phone.

"Your husband can't cover it?"

She twists her hands together, and I let mine curl into loose fists. I'm not going to touch her. I swear, I'm not going to touch her.

"He wasn't my husband, actually," she says. "He was my fiancé, but he's not anymore. We're over. He left."

Is that right?

"Without leaving enough money to cover the rent? The kind of people who live in this building have second homes in Europe."

Maddie looks at me, her eyes painfully hopeful. "He was

that kind of person. He was going to be, anyway, but I'm not. I hope you know that this isn't a long-term problem. I have a plan to fix it, I just need more time because I wasn't prepared for this. If I go to him, I'm sure he'll simply end the lease, and there's nothing around here that I can afford and that's available. I've been off the market for a couple of years, so it's taking me longer than I thought to find a job."

"Off the market?" Fuck my cock hardens in an instant. *The fuck is wrong with me?*

"Out of the job market. My ex thought it would be better for his career if I focused on philanthropy instead of building my own career, so that's what I did. And I don't regret it. I helped a lot of people, but I'm at a loss at the moment. I paid everything but the five hundred and everyone said that I needed to talk to you."

"What's the exact situation with the rent, Maddie? You can't afford any of it?"

"No, I can afford most of it. I'm five hundred dollars short. And I'll give you anything you want to cover it."

I have to get up and walk out. Her words are a wet dream, and I'd take them in a heartbeat.

She has no idea about the thoughts coming through my head.

"*Anything,*" she insists.

So I look her in the eye. "We can come to an arrangement."

"Oh, thank you. Thank you so much. What kind of

arrangement?"

"I have an idea," I say, intent on extending the payment date or halving her rent. I can barely think though, with the thoughts of her telling me "anything" as if I could simply have anything from her.

My gaze drops to her breasts and I have to admit, I would take whatever she offered.

"If you want me, you can have me however you'd like."

Fuck, this is not something I ever thought I'd do, but the way she's looking at me and the way she makes me feel... Before I can stop myself, I agree to what she's suggesting.

"What exactly is it that you have in mind?"

"I think...I'm not sure. I haven't..."

A moment passes and then I offer in desperation, "A quick fuck then?"

Instantly I regret it. *Quick*? What the fuck was I thinking? And just once?

"You really want me?" she questions, and I can't believe I have any ability to hide it.

"From the moment I saw you in that elevator."

About the Authors

Willow Winters

Thank you so much for reading my romances. I'm just a stay at home Mom and an avid reader turned Author and I couldn't be happier.

I hope you love my books as much as I do!

More by Willow Winters
www.willowwinterswrites.com/books

Amelia Wilde

USA today bestselling author of dangerous contemporary romance and loves it a little too much. She lives in Michigan with her husband and daughters. She spends most of her time typing furiously on an iPad and appreciating the natural splendor of her home state from where she likes it best: inside.

More by Amelia Wilde
www.awilderomance.com/

This is the Discreet Edition so no-one knows what
you are reading.

You can find each edition at

www.willowwinterswrites.com/books